A Time Honoured Killing

A TIME HONOURED KILLING

Love Lives Forever

Samesh Ramjattan

Epiphany Books
Oxford, United Kingdom

Print ISBN – 978-1-64467-814-5

Ebook ISBN – 978-1-64467-815-2

Samesh Ramjattan has a Masters in Business Administration from Oxford Brookes University and prior to becoming a bestselling author was an award-winning restauranteur. He began his career writing film screenplays before his first novel, a self-help spiritual guide *Be Your Higher Self*, followed by the detective thriller entitled *A Time-Honoured Killing* and the sci-fi action adventure trilogy entitled *Beyond*. He lives in Oxford, United Kingdom, and has a passion for cooking and travelling off the beaten track.

Find out more at: www.sameshramjattan.com.

For my Brother,

Yogesh

1

The Independent Police Complaints Commission Courtroom was unusually full with every seat taken and some even standing at the back. Hearings like these had the habit of bringing everyone who had ever had a dispute with the London Metropolitan Police or Scotland Yard, as it was more famously known. The proceedings had been drawn out for weeks on end and the fatigue of bureaucracy was evident on the faces of the entire court, particularly the Officers of the court who went about their mundane duties in their respective boxes. The Chief Prosecutor Miles Munroe stood calm and collected despite the hot summer sweat that plagued everybody else. Miles stood tall, as though he were appointed by a higher sense of justice, the unwavering command of the law elevating his somewhat impish demeanour. He paraded around the court floor like a veteran actor embellishing the carefully chosen role and rehearsed dialogue, calling out:

"The Prosecution calls Narendra Shankar to the stand."

Nick Shankar stood up purposefully and walked from the galleries, displaying a confident swagger in each step, realising that all eyes were on him. He was light skinned, with a hint of cinnamon that complimented a delicately chiselled face and sculpted jet-black hair. He glided toward the dock, his tall and muscular frame filling his debonair suit, stepping before the Bailiff who placed the Bible before him.

"Place your…er, do you need another book? Koran maybe?" the Bailiff stuttered. Nick stared the man down with slight contempt, confirming, "I'm half English."

"Place your," the Bailiff continued eager to get this minor infraction over with and return to his day-dreaming.

Nick placed his hand in the appropriate position and began to slowly mouth the words, "I swear to tell the truth, the whole truth and nothing but the truth…" But found himself hesitating on the final few words. He took a small welcome breath of the stale court-room air and then muttered, "…so help me god".

"Thank you. You may take your seat," the Bailiff said as he hurriedly desisted and returned to his seat. Nick sat down welcoming the relief that accompanied as Miles slowly sauntered up to him. Miles offered a rapacious smile similar to the sharpened teeth a predator might brandish before a kill.

"Mr Shankar, please state your name and rank," he opened.

"Nick Shankar. I mean Narendra Shankar T-D-C. Most people call me Nick," he said casually.

"That's Trainee Detective Constable correct?" Miles enquired further.

"That's right," Nick confirmed, as he sunk into his chair and made himself comfortable. He gazed into the gallery to find his superior Officer, Chief Superintendent Rory McNeil, who sat with a pronounced superiority and permanent stiff upper lip, and Detective Sargent Ron Allen, whose large frame sat hemmed in his seat. Ron caught Nick staring at them and grinned making the courtroom proceedings seem farcical.

Miles had noticed the exchange between the men and this only served to motivate his defamatory tone in the line of questioning.

"On the night of January twelfth, two thousand and twelve, both you and Detective Sargent Ronald Allen, entered the flat of one Tyson Dix, a dealer in narcotics, from Pimlico."

"Yes. That's correct," Nick confirmed as he felt the Prosecutor building toward something, but he was unsure what it was.

"According to the arrest reports, you and D-C Allen had come about this information from a, as you put it, reliable informant, named Carley Banks." Miles stated further, as he began to circle the dock, turning his back to the Detective.

"Yes, that's right."

By this point Miles had returned to the desk where he had been seated and picked up a file and began to scrutinize it. Nick scanned the court once more as the audience waited for Miles' next words.

"Carley Banks, a youth offender with a conviction for dealing Cocaine, not to mention burglary, shoplifting, and assaulting an Officer."

Miles then spun around to face Nick, eager to hear what the Detective's response would be to his next question.

"That Officer of course being you."

Nick had turned his attention inward at the mention of Carley Banks but then looked up to find that Miles was eye-balling him in a blatantly accusatory manner.

"And you would deem her reliable, Constable Shankar?" Miles followed up.

Nick turned his attention again to McNeil and Ron. Both were avoiding him now and Ron was less insolent.

"Carly..." Nick blurted, but then quickly rephrased as the formality of his surroundings begged.

"Miss Banks had spent convictions and had since cleaned up her act. As for assaulting me, I let her off with a caution and she brought me regular information. Tip offs which were more valuable, especially in this case, which checked out."

"Would you describe this relationship as one which was more than just a street snitch?" Mile probed, reallising he had discovered a vulnerability.

"I'm not sure what you mean by that?" Nick retorted defensively. But Miles was preparing to probe even further.

"You and Miss Banks share a close romantic relationship. Isn't that true?" Miles declared moving in to face Nick as they weighed each other up like two determined prize-fighters. The courtroom broke into a mild murmur but not enough to warrant the use of a stern gavel by the Chair of the Commission.

"We are friends. That's all," Nick responded adamantly trying to fend off the underlying implications of collusion and guilt.

"Friends? She was one of Tyson's ex-girls. One whom he beat up so badly, he almost killed her," Miles lauded at the top of his voice. "She had good reason to bring you this information."

Nick maintained his resolve against this obvious chink in his battle armour. He knew he had to rise above this onslaught and sway the court back in his direction. A light sheen of sweat glazed over his brow, but he could not wipe it as this would show weakness. It would demonstrate that he was waning under Miles' line of questioning.

"Tyson was not only a major player in the London drugs trade. C-I-D had been after him for years with no success. I saw an opportunity and I took it!" Nick retorted vehemently. Miles sniggered under his breath as if he was personally appalled by the response. "Did that mean ignoring proper arrest procedure?" Miles asked, but swiftly held his hand to Nick dismissing any kind of response, and quickly stated, "Please tell the court the events of that night and why you alone decided to hold the tactical officers at bay?"

"It's all in the report," Nick snarled defiantly.

Exasperated, Miles turned to the Commissioner, "Surely these proceedings deserve better cooperation from the Detective than this?"

The Commissioner swiftly turned to Nick and belted out sternly, "Detective Constable, the court will not tolerate this sort of behaviour. Please respect these proceedings by answering the Chief Prosecutors question."

Nick squirmed awkwardly in his seat as he realised that his proactive defence had crossed into insolence which he quickly reigned in. He glimpsed McNeil looking back disapprovingly and Ron burying his head in his hands, massaging his agonized forehead. The gravity of this situation began to permeate through the false bravado.

"Tyson lived on the top floor of one of the city's worst tower blocks – drugs, knife crime, robbery – you name it," Nick began humbly. "We had to hold Tactical back, because Tyson paid local hoodie gangs as look outs. If they spotted us in the area, Tyson had enough time to hide any incriminating activity."

Nick began to reflect back to the night in question.

It was Pimlico at night. That night was particularly cold, and he could feel the icy wind invade the spaces between his skin and the layers of clothing. He could remember thinking that he was not cut out for this cold. His father had come from India. Gujarat, he thought but couldn't really be sure despite the countless times his father had bored them to death with the story of his childhood growing up under the British Raj. His father would reminisce about the glorious hot weather and cooking his spicy mutton curry. He would go on about that curry. But for some reason and on some level, Nick related to those stories. He grew up on a council estate not unlike this one, but his father's tales of idyllic warmth seem to captivate and help him escape. Thoughts of his father stayed with him as he followed Ron into the graffiti stained lift. Ron pressed the button and the door ground to a reluctant close.

He remembered the stench of urine crawling up his nose to the point where he could barely tolerate it. But he had to endure. Endure all of this if he wanted to get ahead. And boy did he want to get ahead.

It wasn't long before Ron announced that they were there as they stood before an unexpectedly red-coloured door with the polished brass numbers nine-one-nine smartly mounted in the middle. Nick recalled how the door seemed out of place for such an occupant, almost as if it belonged to a dear sweet old lady resembling one's grandmother. His mind spun into all sorts of detail about the imaginary old woman who should have been in this flat. But then he found himself dismissing his imagination with an authoritative "shut-up". That seemed to do the trick as the imaginary sweet old lady was soon vexed but equally an almost overwhelming fear crept up from the centre of his body and practically froze him solid. Only a firm elbow to the midriff from Ron seemed to release the spectre of fear.

"Ready?" Ron barked. Nick nodded trying to restore his lost confidence. He rolled his shoulders and cracked his neck. Then Ron thumped on the door.

A period of silence followed. Nobody seemed to be coming to the door. This waiting took its toll, exacerbating the fear as Nick's heart began to beat faster. Thoughts began to betray his composure.

Did they have the right place? Was this some kind of set-up? Did Carley betray him?

This time Nick thumped even harder – each strike qualified a hope that things were not about to go wrong.

Nick held his breath as he heard a commotion behind the door and after a minute of fumbling the door opened to reveal a waif-like fourteen-year-old girl. She looked almost emaciated, pale and purple – bruised from years of addiction. She turned and motioned them to enter without any real care as to who they were. The elaborate detection measures that had kept them at bay for so many years didn't seem so elaborate after all.

The girl made her way through the kitchen which had not seen home cooking in decades and Nick's fantasy of a sweet old lady tending a quaint cosy flat was soon dispelled as the decay of fast food cartons, strewn vodka bottles and discarded hypodermic needles became the aesthetic.

The girl eventually led them into the living room, to find a young black man in his mid-twenties, slouched low on a tatty worn out sofa watching a distinctly out of place plasma screen TV. The girl crawled back on-to the sofa next to him.

Nick studied the young man. So, this was Tyson he thought, feeling underwhelmed at the meeting and thinking that he could be mistaken for any kid off the street and not someone who was a criminal kingpin in the making.

Nick and Ron stood before Tyson who barely acknowledged them as they entered. The girl picked up a tinged Crack Pipe off the floor and began to take deep puffs from it. She gasped as the white smoke irradiated her swollen lungs and infected her bloodstream, invoking a coma inducing high. She slid into a cuddle next to

Tyson who elbowed her away, repulsed by the show of affection.

"This is my partner Shank I told you about," Ron announced loudly attempting to get things moving, but his words made no impression as Tyson stayed glued to the TV set. By now Nick's pulse was racing. He couldn't work out whether this was Tyson's inert strategy to try and size them up or that he was so high that he wasn't even aware that they were present. Whichever it was, there seemed to be a pervading sense of foreboding that filled his senses.

"Tyson!" Ron lamented again, breaking through Nick's introspective. He looked at his partner who was equally nervous but demonstrated it in different way. He knew that his partner had a reputation for violence, although he had never directed any of that well-known temper his way.

"Wait a minute blood," Tyson finally uttered.

"We going to do this or what?" Ron urged as his infamous temper rose. But Tyson gave no reply. Ron began to sway as his eyeballs rose in his head like a thermometer about to blow.

"You need to chill!" Tyson said in an animated tone that seemed to bring him to life. He sprang to his feet squaring off equally with Ron. Nick's nervousness reached panic, as he prepared to react to the apparent threat to his partner. But none was forthcoming as Tyson suddenly deflated into a more welcoming demeanour and grabbed Ron's hand in a brotherly bond.

"Shank ma' man," Tyson celebrated as he took Nick's hand in a similar manner and held on. Nick breathed a sigh of relief, confirming that Tyson was sizing him up in some strange ritual that only he was party to.

"You stay here and keep Gina company," Tyson quipped. "Ron and I gotta talk."

Gina smiled wryly at Tyson as he gestured for Ron toward the kitchen. Ron looked back at Nick gesturing for him to accept the cordiality of their unlikely host.

"You want some pipe?" Tyson offered Ron as they left the room.

"No, I'm good," Ron declined.

"Sure? It's some good shit. What about you bruv?" Tyson turned to Nick who had become uneasy at the prospect of being left alone in the room with a drug addicted minor. Nick hesitantly looked at Ron then back at Tyson, realising that by accepting he would be committing a crime and risked failing the Met's random drug testing, not to mention being disciplined and sacked. But then he realised Tyson might take it somewhat personally and he might blow his cover. He decided to throw caution to the wind, "Sure. Why not."

"Gina, you heard the man, give him a hit," Tyson barked to the girl who seemed to disregard his request. That only enraged Tyson and he bellowed, "And clean some of this shit up." There was still blatant disregard from her to which Tyson muttered, "Bitch!" as he disappeared in to the kitchen with Ron.

Nick smiled at Gina as she exhaled a puff of smoke. She was only a few years younger than Carley and Nick couldn't help but think that until recently, Carley had filled a similar role in Tyson's entourage. She wore an old faded floral summer dress that, when it fit a few years ago, held the mark of an expensive high street fashion store. Now it was short enough to expose her panty-less vagina and small but erect breasts as she reclined on the sofa without any care for her dignity. Nick could see that she could have been attractive had the drugs not taken its toll on her looks and her ambition. She was clearly around for his amusement, a sexual plaything trading sex for a high. He had known many girls like her. Guys like Tyson hooked them early straight out of school. Some made it out, some over-dosed and some just disappeared – trafficked into the sex trade. At least Carley made it out. He had made sure of that.

The courtroom had become eerily silent at the sound of his testimony, almost as if they had been in the grubby flat with him experiencing every sight, sound and smell.

"Everything was going to plan until I heard the gunshot," He muttered dolefully.

"And that's when you entered the kitchen?"

Miles asked more considerately this time. Nick looked firmly at Miles as his earlier derring-do faded into a more woeful exchange.

"That's correct," Nick affirmed.

Gina planted the pipe haphazardly in Nick's lap and then looked at him with her brown eyes fully open. Her hands were still clasped around it as he took it. Their hands touched and for a moment a part of her true self made a connection as she looked into his eyes and recognised a forgotten empathy in them. He saw her for who she was and not something to use and discard. But then the illusion of the drugs returned, and the reality of her predicament dawned, "Wanna fuck me?" she said flippantly.

Nick recoiled at the remark, handing her back the pipe. She took it and turned away emotionlessly, drawing on the pipe again. The interaction left no latent emotion and she dismissed the exchange with a callous disregard almost as if she was concluding a failed transaction.

Nick paid no more attention to her remark either and for a moment he settled into melancholic contentedness forgetting that he was on undercover.

An earth-shattering bang dislodged his humble slouch on the sofa and he sprung to his feet. It took far more time for Gina to react, as the danger of the sound echoed through her intoxicated state. A million thoughts raced through his mind, but he could not entertain them at this point and his police training sprang into action just as they said it would at the academy. He sprinted toward the kitchen, bursting through the door with vigour, unprepared for what may lay on the other side.

The small kitchen was empty as he surveyed the room, sloppily kicking through the rubbish. Adrenalin was pumping hard as he noticed two figures struggling on the outside balcony. Tyson was weighed down, pressed up against the steel railing that enclosed the small exterior space nineteen floors up. Ron's overpowering brute strength made the youth cower and no amount of street prowess was going to overcome this temperate behemoth, as he used a combination of power and manipulation. Tyson fought as hard as he tried to fend off Ron's pistol. Nick watched helplessly frozen unsure of what to do, and then almost as if time slowed down, he saw Ron, exerting all his strength further, like a champion wrestler, forcing Tyson and almost breaking him in two, over the barrier. Head first he fell.

The memory was still fresh, as Nick recited it to the courtroom. He felt like the hero in a Greek tragedy coaxing the entranced crowd with a triumphant soliloquy.

"D-C Allen was trying to make the arrest, and, in the struggle, Tyson must have lost his footing and fell..."

Nick paused and agonized over the words,

"…to his death."

"And the girl?" Miles enquired, interrupting Nick's reflection.

"Sorry?"

Miles returned to his table and recited from his file, "Fourteen-year old minor named Gina Mason, shot dead at the scene."

Nick was still flabbergasted by the events before him when he realised that he was not alone. He swung around hastily to see Gina carefully advancing toward him. Confusion rushed through his mind.

Did she see the incident with Tyson? What would be her reaction? Maybe she would see them as rescuers, liberating her from her captors?

But then he realised that this scenario involved none of those things, and as he looked more closely at her she demonstrated a rage filled look of chaos and betrayal and one that was only going to be satisfied by revenge.

Gina smashed the Pipe on an old table and raised it up like a dagger ready to slash the flesh from Nick's body. Nick backed away slowly as the junkie girl swung the jagged glass wildly, snarling and choleric satisfied only to draw blood.

But then he heard a whizz which followed a bang, as a bullet sailed past him and into the chest of Gina. It happened so fast that Nick needed to recompose as he watched her chest burst open from the invasion of the projectile. She was thrown backward, reeling and slamming onto the floor like a lifeless ragdoll.

Nick spun around, shocked. He walked over to her and despite the fact that she tried to kill him, he felt uncontrollable remorse. He wanted pick her up, dust her off and send her home to her heartbroken parents. But she was dead.

Ron marched past him with a thunderous determination, slipping on a pair of latex gloves.

"What just happened? This was supposed to be an arrest?" Nick cried out to a disinterested Ron, who moved around the kitchen tidying up the crime scene.

"We need to get our stories straight. Tactical will be here any second."

"What do you mean? They are both dead!" Nick argued in bewilderment.

"Do what you're told, and everything will be fine," Ron urged as he wiped down areas of the kitchen furniture that he had touched with an old dish rag.

"I'm not doing this!" Nick protested, realising that he was unwillingly sinking into a conspiracy of deception and murder. But Ron's patience and been exhausted and in a desperate rage, he grabbed Nick by the scruff of the neck, and spoke as if spitting venom into his ear.

"Listen you little wanker, you do this the way I say! Or I will make this look like your little mess. It'll hang over the rest of your career," Ron seethed as he let go of Nick, and the words lingered in the air as Nick's lack of choices became apparent. He would have to go along with the bully, this murderer, this corrupt policeman – his partner. What could he do, take on all of Scotland Yard? A Trainee's word against a reputable detective like Ron, a protégé of McNeill? He wouldn't stand a chance.

Ron moved over the dead girl's body and delicately picked up her hand, as she still clutched the broken glass pipe. He skilfully removed it, his knowledge of forensics apparent. He then confronted Nick, holding the sharp glass close to his abdomen.

"Now brace yourself. This is going to hurt," Ron said with anticipation.

"What? Why?" Nick exclaimed with worry.

"The bitch attacked you. We had to shoot her in self-defence," Ron said, his anticipation turning to morbid jubilation.

Miles looked on at Nick absorbing the content of his testimony as Nick stared back at him and then at Ron, who returned his glance with the same jubilant expression he had on that fateful night, but now it morphed into pride. McNeill shared Ron's pride displaying an unusual glimmer of emotion

"She attacked me with the broken pipe," Nick confirmed. The tide of opinion had turned in the courtroom. The occupants looked at him with approval and empathy. To them this was a trainee detective who had risked his life to infiltrate and subdue a known drug dealer and sex groomer. To them he was a monster, a by-product of society's illegitimate offal, not worthy of grief, remorse or guilt. They were happier without him and others like him. He would not be missed and the Met who were risking the lives to get the job done, should have been congratulated and rewarded. It didn't matter that the proper arrest procedure had not been followed or that the detective had acted with unnecessary force. Maybe force is what was necessary. This was a brave new frontier. Nick could read it on everybody's face and despite the resultant conflict from that night, this brazen bending of the rules could work in his favour. He stopped as he looked directly at McNeil and they made a connection. They were both thinking the same thing.

Miles realised that he had lost the sway of the commission, but he took one more stab at the detective.

"A fourteen-year-old? Was she that dangerous that she had to be shot?" Miles declared.

"No…" Nick retorted.

Nick stood up and pulled his shirt from his suit trouser, revealing a slash scar on his abdomen.

"She gave me no choice."

2

McNeil stood proud and proper in his office staring out the enormous glass window that enclosed it. He portrayed a steadfast frame, solid and upright, demonstrating a command that masked his indignant lack of emotion. He filled every inch of his Police dress uniform with a devout poise and retained purpose. To him the uniform was more than professional attire, it was a symbol of a more intrinsic experience – a code that spelled moral order, an antidote for the chaos that seemed to go hand in hand with life in this teeming city. For life could only be served through diligent and rational initiative which stifled the seemingly carefree freewheeling extravagance of the human condition. Passion and emotion were opposite bed fellows to the logical and objective reasoning of his simple constitution. And as far he was concerned, that was how he saw the modern Scotland Yard, a sharpened instrument striking at the heart of an apathetic city.

The sun was setting on what was a tumultuous day and the warmth of the light energised his outlook. He embellished it glowing like a brass statue in magnanimous awe.

Nick knocked gingerly on McNeil's door, almost so softly that it might have been missed, but it was followed by a loud holler that was unmistakably firm, preparing him for the bilious conversation that was to follow. He gulped on his weak saliva and entered, taking a deep breath. Nick was greeted by the back of McNeil who stood gazing out the window. He moved slowly taking in the contents of the meticulous office, unsure whether to speak cordial words to announce his arrival.

"First brush with the I-P-C-C today," McNeil uttered without any need for pleasantries or even the need to face Nick.

"You did well. Kept your nerve," McNeil continued.

"Thank you, sir," Nick responded, still addressing the back of McNeil's head. "Although it's an experience I could have done without." He exclaimed further attempting to make light of this frosty exchange.

"Yes, indeed," McNeil agreed, his demeanour softening. "Hypocrites," he barked further, leaving Nick slightly bewildered.

"I don't follow sir."

"They expect us to uphold rule of law, but to deliver it with the diligence of a parking attendant," McNeil sneered.

"It's getting harder to see where the line is,"

Nick replied, hoping his remark would serve to appease the Chief Superintendent's line of thinking.

"Absolutely. We are in danger of becoming dinosaurs, extinct in the face of a savvier criminal. Democracy. Bureaucracy. These are meant to help us protect the citizen, not those who threaten it."

Nick felt his heart quicken, as a sense of foreboding began to constrict him. Where was McNeil going with this? Although there was nothing he could do but stand silently in the middle of McNeil's glib office and listen.

"I've had my eye on you for a while. Watched you climb the ranks. When I saw you in the dock today, I knew. You have that certain look in your eye. It's a look I use to have once," McNeil declared as he turned to face Nick, with a new-found resolute respect.

"The rules of the game have changed, adapted and we need to adapt with it," McNeil continued as his words began to draw Nick in. "You did well today, kept your wits about you and earned favour. My favour."

Nick's body relaxed as McNeil's words began to massage like a fragrant oil, lubricating his meagre resolve.

"Allen is too much of a blunt instrument – sloppy. He almost exposed himself and exposed us. But you on the other hand…" McNeil waxed, conscious that his words were having the desired effect.

"You are shrewd, cunning and very bright. That's what I could use more of," McNeil exclaimed as he slyly slid a shiny new I.D wallet over his desk toward Nick.

Nick stared at it as though it was salvation freshly served before him. It had an inherent beauty only he knew, satisfying an indescribable inadequacy from somewhere within. A tiny part of him resisted like an innate sixth sense that warned him of the unscrupulous elements that he was soon to be in league with. But his resistance was futile, for this token on McNeil's desk was the endorsement that he needed to fill a very large hole.

"I need detectives who aren't afraid to push the boundaries, to get results. A new Scotland Yard, not just in name only," McNeil continued as he noticed the sudden glint in Nick's eye. Like the devil, he had captured Nick's soul.

"I'm not afraid to push sir. I won't let you down," Nick exclaimed.

"I know you won't. And with that comes a few extra perks. High-profile cases, the big arrests. A career to match that ambition," McNeil affirmed, as he extended his hand to Nick, closing the space between them to seal the deal. "Detective Constable Shankar," McNeil said slowly so that that the words carried reverence.

Nick stared at it and considered the

implications of entering into this arrangement, trying to control his reckless compulsions. But then the lure of the detective badge was overwhelming. He shook McNeil's large hands which seem to envelop his own. But then just as quickly McNeil let go and the warmth of the exchange vanished. He retreated to his neat austere desk. Nick took that as a sign to leave. But the anti-climax of the end of the meeting made no impression on him as he opened the door. He had got what came for.

~

The twilight had yielded to the night light as Nick eloped from the Black Cab that had pulled up the narrow street. He paid the Cabbie promptly not even waiting for his change which delighted the driver. Nick shut the door as the vehicle groaned away and he strolled a short distance to The Green Man, a typically old-fashioned tavern, complete with scuffed woodwork, beer sodden carpets and the characteristic and unmistakable smells that had been festering for a hundred and fifty years.

Nick took no time to push his way through the hordes of patrons squeezed into its tiny recesses, swilling away at frothy cold brews. He rested up against the bar in time to meet the round-faced, bawdy owner Stewart, who was a third-generation publican. "Shank," was all the words that Stewart could muster, not one for chit-chat that existed beyond any talk of Arsenal, his favourite football team. On this subject Stewart could rival any town Cryer presenting detailed analysis, statistics and history. Ordinarily Nick would indulge the dour landlord, but he was in no mood for it, so he met Stewart with the equally cursory, "Stella".

"Sure?" Stewart inquired with surprise.

"Long day," Nick replied.

Stewart disappeared with repugnant disinterest and Nick surveyed the place, carefully studying the inhabitants going about their social engagement. He felt a sense of superiority as he took in each person, regarding each with suspicion, expecting that they should recognise that his was now a powerful office of the law – a full detective. His glory was short lived as Stewart returned with his pint. He paid and grabbed the beverage, sipping its welcome refreshment.

He spotted a recently vacated table in an ideally located quiet area of the pub. Eagerly, he moved to it and sat down. The physical relief soothed his constitution. The events of the day had taken its toll and solitude was a welcome friend.

The beer was going down all too well, and Nick had missed the sensation and comfort it brought like the familiarity of an old lover.

But then she appeared.

She could always find him. Not that he was trying that hard to hide. Something instantly made his heart flutter and blood boil at the same time, a feeling of affection and anger, muddled together in a cocktail of passion. She moved with a disgruntled cacophony, almost as if she was ready to take on whomever stood in her way. She spoke with a fire, her words emanated from smouldering embers that were once the fuel of salacious thoughts. Yet occasionally when he looked into her epic blue eyes, her old charred soul echoed remnants of pure love.

She dressed in dramatic opposites, as though two diametric ideals expressed their disquiet in her choice of wardrobe. Today was no exception. An elegant purple velveteen blouse which would have been quite eloquent had it not been paired with a frilled skirt that looked like it had been butchered to reduce its fore-boding length, compelled to rest in the middle of her athletic thighs. All of it was barely held together with minimal button and zip support, burdened to display as much leg and cleavage as possible, tended by trademark black lace lingerie which spent equal amounts of time on parade as her fake-tanned orange skin.

Nick watched her swagger toward him. As she realised his gaze, she asserted her stride, attempting to present a demeanour that was above her station. She stopped before him with a callous self-assurance, trying to obscure him from everyone else in the world. Whether this was protective or selfish, only she knew.

Nick took a deep breath of her. Perfume mixed with her heady musk and he couldn't tell which was more intoxicating. The scent of Carley Banks was unmistakeable. It invaded his nose like a rapturous potion, awakening a ravenous estranged affection.

"Thought you were done with this place. Done with drink?" Carley sneered.

Nick barely looked up at her as scorn dominated, "I'm not in the mood for it tonight," He retaliated.

"You have such a way with words. Makes it hard for a girl to say no," Carley announced indignantly, matching his contemptuous reaction to her.

"A word you rarely use!" Nick snarled.

Carley scoffed before she pithily replied, "Only with you".

The remark had exasperated Nick as she clearly knew what to say to rile him and he knew that it was inevitable that this exchange would result in him giving in eventually. Other couples might embrace, kiss or even hug when they saw each other, but not them. They needed to have their customary tussle before either succumbed, like two powerful opponents who deep down respected each other, but had to conduct the ritualistic dance of antagonization before the delicately agreed ceasefire. Nick's emotional exhaustion began to weaken his fortifications and his body language displayed signs of a truce.

"So how long are we going to do this for before

you let me sit down?" Carley exclaimed equally eager to end the hostilities.

Nick relented and gestured for her to sit down as he swallowed the rest of his now warm beer. Carley slid in next to him, as a minor calm descended over the both of them.

Carley looked unashamedly at Nick as he toyed with the empty glass, watching the last drop of beer glisten at the bottom. He could not understand how she was capable of getting such passion from him. Even though she made him crazy there was something in a deep, dark place that nobody saw, where he cared for her. He had tried in vain to hide it, and he knew that was what infuriated her, for maybe her reaction was out of a need to hear it. But right now, he could not bring himself to admit it. So, all she got was his disdain. But with uncharacteristic liberality he put his hand into his pocket and removed his new detective badge and placed it on the table proudly.

"Look," Nick declared.

Carley looked at it, considering the gravity of this outcome. She smiled disingenuously through her teeth, trying to be proud of Nick's achievement, but she could not. She knew what this token on the table represented.

"You lied?" she asked with afflicted ruthlessness.

Nick's sense of accomplishment retreated as he turned away from her gaze realising that her intuition had found his vulnerability.

"I had no choice," Nick remarked glumly, squaring up and placing some distance between them.

"No choice? You could have told the truth," Carley offered.

"Truth? Where would that have gotten us?" Nick lambasted as he retracted from her and pushed her away. His actions wounded her, and her hardened exterior shrunk as the agony of heartbreak filled her face. Any other girl would shed a tear, but Carley quickly rallied, substituting anger for anguish.

"Being your snitch could have got me killed. But I did it anyway!" Carley bellowed, attracting the attention of the other patrons.

"Why did you?" Nick questioned.

Carley got to her feet cocooning him from the other patrons. She gazed back at him shaking her head slowly, diffusing her present animosity. This time she could not hold back the emotion and for the first time Nick saw a trembling weakness in her eyes. But he couldn't bring himself to stand up and console her. She retreated defiantly and declared, "I have my reasons." The emotion drowned her words and she stormed off before giving away anymore. Nick watched her leave until her figure had vanished in the crowd. A peculiar anxiety had come over him. For the first time he missed her, and he felt the compulsion to chase after her.

In his pocket, his mobile phone rang. He

removed it and studied the screen, then answered
the call.

3

The busy activity of the police and ambulance crews obscured the otherwise drab street. Nick pulled up and parked his unmarked car away from the commotion and quickly alighted. He studied the scene as he approached. The street had been cordoned off in typical operational procedure. However, there seemed a larger than usual complement of officers on the scene especially in this part of the city. Nick slowed his pace down as his instinct told him that that this was no ordinary scene. Whatever had happened was important. The fatigue of this day began to paralyse his already exhausted body. He wished that it could end, and he could find some solace in the comfort of his snug bed. But then he sobered up as he reached the crowds of onlookers that had gathered treating the crime scene like a morbid reality TV show.

Nick made his way through the uncooperative bystanders and then flashed his newly acquired badge to a Constable responsible for crowd control. The Constable quickly permitted him through the makeshift police tape barrier and he marched up to the Constable in charge.

"Evening Constable. What do we have?" Nick said professionally.

"Body sir. Second floor flat. East block, number 14," The Constable replied, with an unusually formal tone.

"Forensics on the scene?" Nick enquired with removed brevity.

"Got here twenty minutes ago sir," the Constable confirmed as Nick began to indignantly survey the street and the onlookers.

The street resembled any other council in London, dominated on either side by red-brick rows of flats and tenements, eroded by the urban decay and tinted by invasive orange street lighting, dispelling any intended quaintness. The streets seemed to tell the stories of its occupant's strife, echoing the repression of hearts and minds in the form of graffiti and waste.

Nick knew this life all too well. He grew up in a street and neighbourhood similar to this. He felt strangely comforted by the blatant realism of it, unthreatened by its ominous danger. Although he would have regarded the police in his neighbourhood with unashamed animosity hurling abusive slogans and standing in opposition to the social obedience and conformity that the uniform signified. The nostalgic thoughts of rebellion brought a strange whiff of excitement and empowerment. But this soon dissipated as he reminded himself which side he stood on now.

Nick returned his gaze to the street and the onlookers who seemed to concoct their own drama of the event, asking and answering their own questions, as if they were amateur detectives providing their own interpretations of what had transpired. His scan of the crowd came to a halt on one face. It belonged to a young man of middle-eastern descent. He seemed unfazed by the bystander drama, almost significant by his stance. His face was demure and doleful, as though it contained an expression of will. He was handsome, with light brown skin, dark brown eyes and defined facial features that benefitted from a pronounced cleft and sculpted cheek bones. He stood with prominence, a manner that separated him from the crowd. He had his eyes fixed on Nick almost with an intention of purposeful connection. Nick continued to scan the rest of the crowd, attempting to exhibit casual nonchalance, but the man remained fixed on him.

"Any witness statements?" Nick enquired softly.

"Few sir, but this area is full of Fugees sir…" the Constable blurted, but then apprehensively rephrased as he noted Nick's disapproval, "Foreigners sir, Afghans, Iraqi, little or no English. And those that do, almost never talk to us."

Nick carefully turned to gaze at the man who

seemed so preoccupied with him, but he had vanished. Something told him that he was important. But he wasn't sure why just yet.

For a department that relied on precision and scientific certainty, forensics seemed to conduct themselves with sporadic dishevelment, Nick thought as he entered the flat where even more commotion seemed to ensue than on the street. It seemed as if the entire forensics team had vacated the comfort of their congenial laboratory and were deployed in this tiny little flat. With so many personnel on the scene, it made it difficult to process the scene without contaminating it.

Nick strolled through the flat cautiously, mentally recording the environment, often taking in elements that others missed. His ability to meticulously record a scene was what made him progress through the ranks so voraciously. He saw what others didn't. Everything else in his life might have been shrouded in confusion but when he worked, a certain clarity pervaded. He could get the job done better than the rest. And they knew it.

Nick came up behind a short balding portly man who wouldn't seem out of place meddling in grease and oil in a car garage. He wore a plain grey suit that seemed to be his only one and it had never seen the sanctity of a dry-cleaner, sporting the irreverent stains from pies and cheap instant coffee – two things that this Scots-man could not get enough of.

"Pulling overtime, Charlie? Nick announced as he surprised the man.

Charlie irked slightly as he swung around to see Nick grinning.

"I'll say. Missing the game n'all," Charlie complained as he shook Nick's extended hand, directing Nick further into the flat.

"They stuck you with this one, did they?" Charlie jested.

"Yeah. Why?" Nick asked, perplexed by the remark.

"Nothing. 9-9-9 call came in at eight seventeen, from the phone box on the street," Charlie continued, glossing over the remark.

"Who from? Neighbours?" Nick probed.

"Unknown," Charlie retorted hastily.

"We need a transcript of the call." Nick remarked, recalling his training.

"This isn't *our* first case, detective," Charlie responded sarcastically, then impatiently continued, "Council records indicate the flat as being occupied by a Syrian family. But they moved out 3 months ago. Since then witnesses claim they've seen a young Islamic male aged in his early twenties, coming and going occasionally with the victim. The words resonated with Nick, whose attention became instantly aroused.

"Early twenties?" Nick inquired.

"That's what they claim," Charlie answered becoming irritated by Nick's interruptions.

"Victim?" Nick exclaimed, suddenly aware of

Charlie's annoyance. Charlie exhaled in a pronounced huff and pushed through in to the flat's bedroom.

The bedroom had last seen decoration in the seventies when it had last had occupants who had regarded it as a permanent home. Nick studied the room with fastidious care and attention scanning the peeling wallpaper, worn carpet thread and yellowing paint-work. It was meagrely furnished, with a contrite bed, wardrobe and dressing table that served as adequate comforts. Two of Charlie's men continued to process the scene, one sloppily dusting the furniture for finger prints and the other photographing the evidence.

Nick settled his gaze on the bed at the middle of the room. Cocooned in several layers of white sheets, lay the body of a woman.

Nick began his survey at the base of the bed, with her feet. They were small, pedicured and soft with delicate toes that seem to suggest that she had only worn expensive elegant shoes. His eyes followed her form, absorbing her sumptuous curves, up along her olive coloured calves to the back of her knees. The middle of her body was wrapped in luxurious white sheets that seemed alien in such an environment and more suited to palatial settings. Nick completed his survey at the top of her head, which was buried face down in the bosom of forgiving pillows and blood-soaked sheets that enshrouded her in an aura of death.

"Victim is a twenty-five-year-old Muslim woman, but no positive I-D yet," Charlie continued as Nick seemed engrossed by the body.

"Local?" Nick inquired.

"No. Neighbours claim they don't know who she is, only that they saw her come and go with the possible suspect."

Nick looked at the body once more and a feeling of sadness descended over him as the brutality of the scene dawned on him. He remembered his training – to keep emotion at bay and remain focused to the profession. But fatigue had begun to take its toll and the fate of this nameless victim seemed to pierce his invulnerable exterior. He turned his attention to her once more, moving in close and placing his hand on the bed. Then he extended his fingers and touched the skin of the corpse. Something stirred within him. Something was different here. This lifeless corpse spoke to him as if she was still alive with oxygen and blood coursing through her veins.

Nick hastily removed his hand from her, focusing back on his investigation, scouring the rest of the crime scene. He removed a pen and gently inspected her clothing as it lay neatly placed on the dressing table. Then, contrary to protocol, he stroked the victim's clothing and the smooth texture evoked a sense of who she was. Across the room in a corner stood a solitary shoe. Nick slowly moved over to it and knelt down inspecting it, noting its brand. Beside the shoe, blood was splattered across the wall and wardrobe. Nick peered inside the wardrobe, carefully holding the handle with his sleeves. Inside was an arrangement of cheap second-hand clothing – all men's. On the floor, beside the wardrobe lay an ominous black granite block with an elaborate Islamic inscription carved into it. Along the edge and corner, dried blood and mottled hair clung to it.

"Blunt force trauma?" Nick asked, pivoting his head up to Charlie as he spoke.

"And the inscription?" Charlie enquired.

"Islam is a mercy. If you see the opposite – cruelty. Then it is not Islam," Nick read, much to the surprise of Charlie and the two forensic officers.

"I remember seeing it as a child," Nick said coyly, as Charlie rolled his eyes in disinterest.

"What do you think?" Charlie questioned attempting to test the young detective. Nick stared back at Charlie and the officers realising that they were sizing his knowledge up. Nick took a deep breath and looked around the room once more, finalising his impressions.

"She was killed over here and then moved to the bed. She was dressed at the time of the murder. The killer confronted her, there was a struggle and she was struck…to the left side of her temple. But she didn't die straight away," Nick delivered confidently, animatedly prancing about the room.

"The killer had to strike her again, this time to the back of the head, and that was the fatal blow. She's a stranger to these parts, judging by her clothing and shoes – all expensive. She's used to a life of pampering."

Nick moved in closer to the victim, almost as if he was talking to her disconnected soul beyond the heavens. Charlie and the officers remained intrigued at Nick's natural prowess for deduction.

"She knew her killer. No forced entry and she didn't run, she stood up to him. He took time to undress her and wrap her in the sheets, face down so he didn't have to face her, showing us, he felt some remorse, shame even," Nick continued. "The killer was trying to make a statement."

"Jealousy? Boyfriend or husband perhaps," Charlie intimated, trying not to let Nick claim all the limelight.

"Boyfriend maybe. She doesn't look like she would marry into this life," Nick claimed quietly.

"Bound to be fluids. Let's turn her around," Charlie declared bluntly.

Nick moved slightly out of the way as the two Forensic Officers shifted in over the bed and placed their strong arms under the lifeless body of the victim. Then with surprising care they gently turned the body around revelling her face. Nick's curiosity was at fever pitch as he sought to place a face to his diligently crafted deductions. Slowly he moved in with a mild excitement, focusing on her unveiled face as the two burly officers retreated after their menial task.

Her head had gently slid to one side as one arm lay trapped underneath it. The other folded over casually resting over chest almost as if she were alive and leisurely turned over from topless sunbathing, nonchalantly covering her rounded full bosom and concealing her small pert light brown nipples. Her eyes had remained open. They were translucent white with dark, soulful centres, which seemed to stare hauntingly back at the occupants of the room. For all who stared back at her time was frozen, as if she held them in the beguiling spell with those eyes that seem to mesmerise and tell a story. A story of tragedy and pain painted in lurid oils of beauty and grace.

Nick glimpsed her face just as the forensic officer flashed a series of shots, bathing the room in an electric blue. With each successive flash, the shock and awe of the scene sent a current of cold shivers through his spine. It seemed like a dream that quickly graduated into a horror. His breathing seemed to stop as the shock permeated and began to freeze the function of his body, emotion and thought. All he could see before him was her face transfixed and locked in a steely exchange. The cold professional execution with which he had dissected her livelihood had come crashing to the floor, lying alongside the same pool of blood in the carpet. He fell to his knees as the will was exiled from his body. She was more than a faceless victim now. The memories of everything that she meant to him came flooding back like an unwelcome spectre, reclaiming his deflated heart. He had known so much of her in life and now here she lay – dead.

"You know her?" Charlie asked gravely.

Nick's head sunk, trying to hold back emotion and regain his composure. He looked at her lost in her helpless gaze staring at a Gold Heart Locket chain around her neck, that held so much meaning for him.

"Khan. Her name is Adilaah Khan," Nick announced bleakly.

4

Nick sat huddled on a solid upholstered wooden bench in the busy office hallway. He slouched awkwardly across its uncomfortable solid frame watching as the officers and clerical staff went about their business, criss-crossing him on their morning errands. To him their streaks of movement resembled rough broad-brush strokes on an uneven canvas. His head was drenched in furtive thoughts of the last twenty-four hours. He had had little sleep and his body struggled under the heavy burden of fatigue. But his physical state didn't affect him. He was too consumed by the haunting images of Adilaah Khan. He closed his eyes momentarily and his thoughts evacuated into a blackness, thick and consuming. Memories of Adilaah's illuminated form permeated the black fog, and immediately he was transported back to her. They felt so strong. So real. In this etheric world he reached out and touched her, laying his hand gently on her soft delicate olive skin, caressing her as he felt the warmth of blood and life coursing through her body, not the vacant corpse he witnessed only hours earlier. Her face drifted up in front of his, and he was so close to her he could touch it. An old and dormant feeling enveloped him like a familiar heavy quilt. Nick accepted it, unable to fight the feeling.

Beams of liberating sunlight filtered through the large windows bathing Nick's meditative state and as the energising glow of orange illuminated him, he opened his eyes, returning to the office hallway and temporarily exorcising the lingering ghost of Adilaah.

"Congratulations on your promotion," Nick heard the words as he sat up noticing that Miles had taken an overbearing position over him.

"Thanks," Nick muttered as he thoroughly composed himself to a more professional standing.

"Long night?" Miles probed somewhat condescendingly, gazing over his anguished demeanour.

"You could say that," Nick replied humbly, avoiding the direct gaze that Miles had employed, ironing out the creases in his sloppy attire.

"Running before you can walk, aren't you?" Miles offered, as Nick looked perplexed, but too exhausted to take any offence.

"The Khan murder?" Miles tested, "The Superintendent has seemingly great aspirations for you."

"I'm sure," Nick answered, suddenly aware that Miles had an agenda.

"There's only one problem though..." Miles

retorted quickly, "When those aspirations get in the way of what we do here."

Nick froze his gaze on Mile's accusatory stare, feeling the cold weight of his tone.

"Serving the law," Miles finished.

Further down the hall, McNeil appeared in front of his office door and caught sight of the exchange between Miles and Nick. The two men turned to face him, Miles relishing the exchange as an opportunity to instil doubt in McNeill's perceptions.

"Remember my door is always open," Miles quipped before retreated from Nick, and walking in the direction of McNeil.

"Superintendent," Miles uttered a cursory greeting at McNeil as he passed by. "Miles," McNeil muttered distastefully, barely acknowledging the man.

Miles' words resonated with Nick as he realised that he may have misjudged Miles' intentions. All this time he had believed that Miles had concocted some kind of misplaced vendetta against the young detective, perhaps because he distrusted the speed and circumstance in his rise through the ranks. Indeed, he had known Miles for having a by the book reputation that did not always sit well with most of the people in Scotland Yard, but it was a respected reputation nevertheless, one that was earned diligently, even though they did not exactly see eye to eye. Nick now felt as though the Prosecutor was trying to throw him a life-line and not see him drown without one. Although at that moment he couldn't trust the conflicting and opposing thoughts going through his mind.

"You need to make this quick, I have a Press conference about the Khan murder in ten minutes," McNeil barked at him as he entered his office, clearly irritated by Nick's appearance.

"Well sir. That's precisely why I'm here – the Khan murder," Nick spoke amiably.

"What about it?" McNeill retorted shortly.

"This is a bit embarrassing sir, but…" Nick hesitated, trying hard to find a diplomatic word, "I have a conflict of interest…"

"You knew the victim," McNeil blurted bluntly, as the knowledge of which surprised Nick, who only be-came more agitated.

"Since she was a child," Nick replied.

McNeil stopped his activity behind the desk and came up face to face with Nick. "You knew her and her family. Give this case the justice it deserves," He waxed convincingly.

Nick shuddered as he hesitantly uttered, "No-body…nobody knew about us," Nick gulped. "Romantically, I mean."

But McNeil was hearing none of it. "And nobody needs know," McNeill reassured.

"Her father is one of the P-M's closest advisers. So, we need to handle this with delicacy. He's a man who values his privacy. The last thing they want to see is their daughter's honour and reputation dragged through the mud," McNeill continued.

Nick's protest was waning under McNeill's coaxing argument. The emotional and physical fatigue had begun to take its toll and he felt like he could collapse at any moment.

"Nick, handle this with the right amount of tact and there's no limit to where you could go," McNeill exclaimed as though there was nothing left to discuss. He then turned around and headed back to his desk.

Nick stood motionless for a moment and suddenly felt the urge to flee, throwing the detective badge at his manipulative boss in the process. But he resisted the wily temptation with unwitting restraint. McNeill looked at him once more with a pronounced frown.

"That will be all," he declared, and that signalled the end of their engagement. Nick turned solemnly and made for the door. But then McNeill had more words for him, "Oh, one more thing, D-C Shankar."

Nick froze and turned around unwillingly facing the Superintendent.

"I'd be careful what you say to the Prosecutor. He doesn't share my vision of this department. Tread carefully, for your sake," McNeill warned with a veiled threat underlying his advice.

Nick could think of nothing better than to retire to an invigorating shower and the welcoming embrace of his bed covers. The temptation would have been enough on any other normal day. But then again, he couldn't remember that last time he had encountered a normal day. He was becoming convinced that in this job normal days did not really exist. Everywhere he looked he was haunted by the image of Adilaah's ghost. He saw her in the reflection of the running water at the bottom of the sink, in the glass windows and doors and in the memory of shared cups of coffee while he drank his in the staff canteen. Most of all the unbearable weight of despair that had overwhelmed the alcoves of his heart. He felt the guilt of responsibility. She was dead and somehow, he felt he was to blame. It was this feeling that motivated him to venture down the various flights of stairs of the bleak stairwell to the basement housing the Coroner, eagerly avoiding the busy elevator that meant interaction with other officers, something his melancholy did not permit.

Reluctantly Nick approached the large glass screen that was the window into the Coroner's laboratory. The laboratory's cold white tiles and sterile stainless-steel surfaces were obscured by the bright trio of spotlights that beamed down in the middle of the room, over lighting the sculptured steely examination table. Across the table lay Adilaah's rigid body, unceremoniously naked without any dignified cover. Nick analysed her figure which in life was shapely and desirable.

Now its pale grey stiffness signified her mortal end.

The Assistant Coroner, Aisha moved in closer, completing her mandatory clinical autopsy, inspecting her body for clues as to the cause of death, periodically speaking into a voice recorder and taking photographic evidence. As she concluded, she noticed Nick in the observation window and deliberately ignored him.

As Nick entered the laboratory, he found Aisha perched in front of her desk, preparing to transpose her voice recordings. She saw his emergence has an unwelcome interruption of her work. Aisha had a small frame with black, fiercely platted hair that was better suited to a six-year old. Today she wore a bland ensemble that consisted of a white t-shirt that highlighted a flat chest over a pair of tailored trousers and flat soulless shoes, all trapped under an oversized lab coat. She had an insipid personality to match her plain choice of clothing. She belonged in the laboratory. Nick plonked himself into an accompanying seat next to her. He stared at her in an attempt to get her attention which she was irked to grant.

"Did you establish the cause of death?" Nick inquired.

"Yes," she blurted.

"And?" Nick persisted.

"It will be in the report Nick!" Aisha declared.

"Just today, can you forget procedure and think

of the victim. Please?" Nick pleaded, hoping her sense of humility would pervade.

"Blunt force trauma to two sections of the head. At the frontal lobe and at the back of the head, at the base of the skull. Induced an acute subdural haematoma. She was dead in a matter of minutes," Aisha sprouted off, with a slightly banal tone that was suited to a specimen and not a person.

"Any foreign fluids?" Nick probed further.

"She wasn't raped if that's what you're asking," Aisha patronised. "But her stomach contents did exhibit an unusual number of anti-depressants." Nick paused to process Aisha's words, and then lifted his gaze to Adilaah's body. It was difficult to see her in that state especially after the visions that had plagued him all morning. He felt as though she could open her eyes at any moment and stare back at his all-consuming gaze.

"You OK?" Aisha asked with uncharacteristic empathy.

"Anything else?" Nick retorted, bluntly dismissing her offer, prompting Aisha to tense up and return to her cool disposition.

"One more thing. I found traces of a strange compound present in her uterus," Aisha exclaimed.

"What kind of compound?" Nick inquired with intrigue.

"I'm not sure. I'll have to run a few tests – might take a few hours," Aisha said curtly.

"Be sure and call me only," Nick said

ominously, leaving Aisha puzzled by the remark. She disregarded it and returned diligently to her work. "Aisha", Nick said commandingly, prompting her to look him in the eye, eager to hear what would follow, so that she might dismiss it with blithe indifference.

"Thanks," Nick uttered with heartfelt gratitude, which caught Aisha by surprise. She smiled, blushing indiscriminately.

5

The prayer hall of the mosque was grand, with high vaulted ceilings and ornate carvings of ancient Islamic scripture. Nick couldn't help but feel somewhat humbled by the imposing structure. A few hours of sleep, an invigorating shower and change of clothes made him feel altogether more lucid and focused. He had ditched the suit which he had spent almost forty-eight hours in, and settled for denim jeans, white t-shirt, trainers and black jacket, attire more fitting of his need for comfort than presentation.

By now the sun was directly overhead ensconcing the building in liberating white light and awakening the nuggets of coloured glass embedded in the ivory plaster, meant to resemble the gemstones in the original ancient mosques of the middle east.

Nick stood quietly and patiently to the rear of the hall. Before him sat rows of engrossed Muslim men, perched upon their multi-coloured mats and transfixed by the figure on stage. Each were dressed in their traditional Thawabs – long cotton tunics and adorning white prayer caps;

demonstrating their devout humility to their god. Nick followed the neat converging lines clocking each one's face. Somehow, he envied their blind subscription to their faith, eager to hear some revelation that might assist in their individual journeys towards salvation. He wished he found similar revelation in such words. For there were those times when all of the assertion and thoughts that his overworked mind could muster, brought no solace and indeed, like with anybody, he felt there was the need for a stronger and altogether more omni-present tonic. These were the times when his choices made no sense and he then wondered how he found himself at that present point in his life, questioning all of it – Carley, McNeill, Ron and of course Adilaah, and how badly things had been left with her. The thoughts spun around incessantly until he felt the weight of the words of the speaker on stage.

"It is now time to awake from your trance…" the words echoed. Nick felt as though they were intended only for him.

"This is a time of great suffering for all Muslims around the world. For many brothers of the Holy Prophet, our faith is under treat," the speaker continued with voracious conviction. "Threatened by a war of attrition waged by enemies of our faith. Many of us would label them Infidels, but I do not."

He then paused and surveyed his engrossed audience.

"The enemies of our faith exist only in our own hearts!" He announced with passion. "And no heart can be vanquished, if it is true!" Another solemn pause left the crowd desperate for the closing words. "Search inside your own hearts and find your truth. God be with you!" He finished.

Rapturous applause followed his words as the hall was consumed by heartfelt adoration. Nick felt compelled to clap and gave a slow-handed applause as he watched the speaker descend from the podium, greeting and glad-handing the congratulatory pious Imams and Clerics. Nick began to walk closer to the stage closing in on the white-haired speaker, cloaked head to toe in white and gold patterned robes which made him seem supremely benevolent and avuncular.

Nick could remember how, as a child his robes would bedazzle him, garnering only admiration and humbled respect. To him the man had a peculiar untold wisdom which seemed to calm him, making demands on his sub-conscious self to live up to a higher set of morals. At first sight his very presence seemed to terrify him, forcing him to take refuge in his father's shadow, but there was something about the man's invoking spirit that would welcome him in, like an enveloping embrace that he craved. Indeed, after that initial looming shock, Mahmoud Khan felt like the father he wanted.

Mahmoud caught sight of Nick, as his admirers

began to wane and made a determined march in his direction. The acknowledgement filled Nick with an elevating excitement.

"Did you enjoy the speech?" The words came from nowhere with an underlying derisive tone. Nick turned around to discover the presence of a young Muslim of muscular build, dark brown skin, large sunken eyes, short buzz-cut hair and meticulously manicured beard.

"Ashraf," Nick offered a frosty greeting that held none of the eminence that he had felt for Mahmoud. "Your father still has a way with words."

"What do you want?" Ashraf inquired bluntly.

"I'm meeting your father," Nick replied confidently. Ashraf stared back at Nick with a resolute disdain. He could sense Ashraf's annoyance as he cast his mind back to a time when the two were boys and they shared an inseparable bond, despite their differing religious backgrounds.

Nick recalled first driving up to the enormous house that stood high on Muswell Hill, set back from the tree-flanked road, and connected via an asphalt driveway that was shrouded by elegant multi-coloured flower beds. He could just about see out the front passenger side window while drowning in the maroon leather upholstered seats, careening his neck to take in all of the splendour of the house and its palatial gardens. His father encouraged him to sit down more appropriately as the brand new 1990 black Jaguar Sovereign came to a serene halt in front of the house. His father disembarked promptly, and Nick watched as he went up a minor flight of stairs and into the house. Nick looked about, but his boyish curiosity could not be abated, and he opened the large car door, unclipped the seat belt and alighted from the car. Nick could not understand how his father's boss could afford all this by selling fabric. He must have sold a lot to be able to afford this house, these gardens and a driver, in the form of his father to drive him around all day in an expensive car. A lot of fabric indeed!

Nick walked along the side of the house, absorbing the tidy white washed walls that aligned the renovated Victorian mansion and symptomatic bay windows. In one of them stood a girl only a few years younger than him. The sun irradiated her pale, milky complexion and highlighted her stifled gaze from out the window. She looked enviously at him, longing for the freedom of fresh air, sunlight and the joy of opening up her lungs, while racing through the garden on the liberating damp green grass. She gave Nick a hopeful wave as she turned toward him, giving him her full attention. The sunlight ensconced her tiny frame making her look like an angel. Nick smiled at her and she returned the gesture, presenting a momentary fleeting gleefulness. But then that was soon gone as she turned her attention back at her original preoccupation.

Nick followed her stare and entered into a densely planted enclosure. A short distance away, he watched as a boy of similar age plundered away at numerous tennis balls strewn across the lawn with a cricket bat. He placed a determined amount of vigour in smacking the daylights out of each ball that nested peacefully in the grass. He continued for a while as Nick watched with a particular feeling of delight, sharing the same sense of joy that the little boy shared as he pummelled them.

The boy slammed another unsuspecting ball and it whizzed past Nick's feet. The boy ceased his activity and began to gaze at Nick. Nick then summarily picked the ball up and tossed it back to the boy, who lifted his bat up and smashed it in the opposite direction. Nick then searched around for another ball and upon discovering one buried in a flower bed, tossed it with more skill and velocity than the previous. This time the boy put far more batting skill into his response and thudded it straight back to Nick with some height. Nick quickly positioned himself under the falling ball and with the ceremony of a world-class cricketing fielder, caught it and held it up triumphantly. He gazed back in the direction of the boy who chuckled at the display, then motioned for him to come over. Nick strolled over cautiously and stopped in front of him.

"Ashraf," he said, extending his small hands, dropping the bat.

"Narendra," Nick replied cordially. "But everyone calls me Nick."

Nick still saw that boy in the man before him, but Ashraf had changed. That little boy had grown into a man that had always struggled to emerge from under his father's shadow. He had forged his entire character with reverence to his father's will and he had become bitter that his father did not recognise it. In fact, Mahmoud took it for granted and toyed with his love, withholding it so that he could maintain the control over the boy who had evolved into a man, but who was still desperate for his father's love. Nick felt empathy for him for they shared the same estranged relationships with their fathers, and perhaps that was what brought them together initially. Two boys whose friendship was forged in the absence of sentiment of love from their fathers. That, however may have been the way things were, but now things were very different. That friendship had died a long time ago and now all that was left was a disgruntled acquaintance moulded on a previous incarnation. Now their exchange was one of hostility, two adversaries with opposing ideals.

"I'm sorry about Adilaah," Nick offered, as his own grief was hoping to make amends with

Ashraf's. But it did not seem to, as Ashraf retorted, "One of those things."

"She will get the justice that she deserves," Nick reassured.

"She will. We will see to it. Without interference," Ashraf sneered.

"Ashraf!" Mahmoud's voice commanded as he appeared before them. His presence made Ashraf immediately desist. "Go and attend to your duties, while I speak to Narendra."

Ashraf looked at his father defeated, then scowled at Nick and walked off in a huff.

"Narendra, how have you been, my child?" Mahmoud lamented with a welcoming tone, genuinely thrilled to see him. Nick beamed at the gesture, uttering, "Fine sir. How are you?" Extending his hand for Mahmoud to shake.

"You are not too big for me to give you a hug!" Mahmoud lauded as he wrapped his big arms over Nick shrouding him in affection. Nick tried to maintain his composed exterior, but the old man's kindness overcame him, and he obliged.

"Let's go walk in the garden," Mahmoud gestured, and they strolled through to a pristinely manicured garden that sat beside the mosque in a walled enclosure.

Nick and Mahmoud strolled along a ceramic tiled path that snaked its way through the sun-baked garden flanked by the heady perfume of roses.

"I didn't think you'd be speaking so soon

after..." Nick hesitated. "Adilaah." Nick glanced over at the tall man and he noticed the mention of his daughter's name weakened his resolve.

"It takes my mind off of the situation and allows me to focus on my faith. You know Allah gives us these tests in life to make us stronger and bring us closer to him," Mahmoud affirmed. "Have you seen your father?"

"Not Lately," Nick answered, afflicted by the mention of his father.

"A child should never forget the sacrifices that a parent makes for him. You should honour him while you still can," Mahmoud advised.

"He barely remembers who I am," Nick replied with deepened remorse.

They had come to the end of the small garden, and Mahmoud stopped, slowly turning to face him. He paused and took a solemn breath as he spoke. "That is why I asked for you to come here today. I've known you all your life, just as I have known your father and I am certain you are the kind of man who will honour my family especially with this investigation."

"Of course. I'll do my best for you," Nick reassured as Mahmoud placed both his hands on Nick's shoulders, conveying the weight of his words upon him.

"I know you and Adilaah were friends from a young age, and you want to do right by her by bringing her murderer to justice, but she wasn't perfect. She made plenty of mistakes in her life and bringing those mistakes into the public eye, will only serve to damage her memory," Mahmoud reasoned.

"I'm not sure what you want of me?" Nick asked, searching for clarity in the request.

"I'm asking for you to honour my daughter's memory by not dredging up her past. I'm asking for you to keep certain things within the family, as though it were *your* family. As if she were *your* sister, and *you* were protecting her honour," Mahmoud pleaded.

Nick contemplated the words of the old man, and he was still unsure what the old man wanted. Of course, he would work tirelessly to ensure that Adilaah's murderer was brought to justice, but he wasn't sure that the justice he wanted was the same that Mahmoud Khan wanted. Mahmoud wanted a justice that meant Adilaah's reputation and indeed his own remained untarnished. But did Adilaah do something that might have already tarnished it? Their relationship was a well-kept secret – Adilaah saw to that. But was this the same girl he once knew, or like Ashraf did she too evolve into something that was unsavoury and somewhat warped, hiding her indiscretions from behind a hidden world that he was only slightly privy to. Was this the reason that such a high-ranking case was tossed in his relatively naïve lap so quickly, so that he would fail, and no one would be the wiser, then the world would just carry on the way it is? Unresolved and uninterrupted. The questions began to overwhelm and create anxiety, swirling about his mind. He could use a drink, but then that would do him no good.

6

Nick could remember distinctly the next time he saw her. It was three years ago. She was no longer that little bird in the sun-drenched window, longing for freedom from within the Khan mansion. She had grown into a majestic, graceful swan emanating an aura of pure angelic white. She had a full and voluptuous figure, endowed with ample heaving breasts and generous peach shaped rear, all shrouded beneath a flowing pale green and shimmering gold Salwar Kameez. The silk made her movements seem effortless, as if she glided amongst those around her, who instantly became smitten by her beauty, adoring her benevolent presence.

The boredom of the ageless ceremony had set in and as it was customary at all Indian weddings, large portions of the male attendees had congregated in the hotel bar, leaving behind frustrated woman folk who had the customary task of child minding and idle gossip. The Pundit had managed to make it into his second hour of incongruent Sanskrit chants that barely held the consciousness of the bride and groom, let alone the audience of well-wishers. The Hawan fire pit had reached epic proportions filling the hall with acrid grey smoke created by the fuel of butter-ghee, mango sticks and camphor, meant to signify blessing but instead tempting the fire alarm and staining the interior decoration of the opulent five-star building.

Nick swallowed the double Jameson's with sanguine determination, taking refuge in its sweet burning sensation as it disappeared down his throat. Whisky was the drink of choice at most Indian weddings and they would certainly go through a few cases tonight before the ensuing hazy debauchery and accusatory chaos. Nick was tempted to get another drink, but he resisted the temptation, reminding himself of his role as usher to his poor cousin – the groom on stage.

Perhaps the belt of whisky alerted his senses in the noisy nuptials, but he spotted her from the bar, making her way to the table in the adjoining hall. Her presence haunted the mundane dutiful actions as his gaze seemed fixated on her and nothing else. He found himself gravitating slowly towards her, almost as if he was powerless to the force she emitted, pulling him toward her. The rows of patterned Saris and striped Suits lead to her like a serenading pathway. As she settled in she looked around, and then just as indiscriminately, she caught sight of him too. And for a brief moment the whole room seemed silent and still, and they were all alone. Something stirred deep down, and they wanted to retreat to their individual lives, but something kept them fixated on each other.

But then his family yanked him back to reality and back to his duties. Nick looked back at her, trying to maintain his connection. She watched him too, slightly bemused.

Nick was ushered up on stage for the next phase in the laborious ceremony. This part was simple, and had he not been so flummoxed by the gaze of one person in particular, he would have not got it wrong. It was traditional for each side of the family to place garlands on one's opposite number, in order to welcome them into the family. It was simple. Nick was handed the surprisingly heavy orange Marigold garland and stood third in the queue to complete his part of the ritual. But then he fixed his gaze on her once more, while she tried to hide the all too obvious attention by drooping her head coyly. Nick moved up to his turn, as she propped her head up and stared back at him. He felt the magnetic connection and outstretched his arms, attempting to complete his duties as he kept his eyes on her. Suddenly the hall erupted in laughter, which included his admirer. That prompted him to shift his attention, and then he realised it. He had gone left instead of right and placed the garland on a rather befuddled priest. Quickly he removed it and placed it over the correct person in his soon to be cousin's family, apologising for the indiscretion. The crowd appointed a chuckle and small applause at the welcome comic relief in such a monotonous affair.

Nick had managed to pry himself away from the family commitments that entangled him for at least another hour. By then the bar had become impassable, roaring with festivity and raucous merriment. He had searched around for her to no avail, and he succumbed with disappointment, realising that she must have gone home. The overwhelming tug of war of family introductions had taken his toll and he was no longer able to submit to any more meetings of long lost aunts and uncles he had never before met, nor endure the inadvertent match making with would be suitors. He decided to slope off to a quiet protracted area of the hotel. He had heard that the hotel had a rooftop pool and bar with outstanding views over the Thames river, so he thought he would explore.

The elevator opened to a minimalist glass, steel and concrete pool area, apportioned with generous potted palm trees, surrounding a neat symmetry of aligned sun loungers and cocktail tables. Royalty or celebrities would not be out of place up here, and it was a world apart from the rowdy coloured pastiche that was the Indian wedding carrying on downstairs.

The all too eager bartender offered Nick a drink as he strolled into the enclosed bar area, but before he could indulge, something caught his eye at the end of the pool, seated on the last two sun loungers. He ventured further, emerging from the covered glass enclosure and into the open air. The sound of errant giggling muffled the sombre flow of running water that made its way into the pool, trying to emulate some sort of contrived paradise.

Nick approached slyly, hoping his intrusion might not offend and be met with scorn. As he stopped before the last two sun loungers, he saw her – sprawled across the lounger that usually accommodated slinky swimsuits rather than elaborate Asian formalwear. She had a degree of casual disregard, a carefree reproach that he had not noticed before. She giggled with bubbly delight, sounds of joy that seemed to compliment her relaxed yet elegant poise. She did not clam up as he stood before them the way her friend did, trying to conceal her half smoked cigarette like it was forbidden contraband. Her eyes greeted him with a gentle alluring welcome, almost as if she was expecting him – the whiff of her alluring scent was meant to knowingly draw him up to this rooftop haven. Her smile graduated to a grin, invoking a sense that she was overjoyed that he persevered and found her.

"Can we help you?" her friend blurted curtly as she realised that she was becoming redundant in the duet that was unfolding.

"I needed some air," Nick said politely to the smoking girl and then looking back at his muse. "I hope I'm not intruding," he continued.

"Not at all," she said eager to dismiss anything her friend might say to ruin the encounter.

Her Hijab had dropped from her head and the V-cut of her Salwar Kameez revealed the top of her sweat glistening breasts, unashamedly teasing his eyes toward areas that were previously off limits.

"This is Fatima," she said, sensing that introductions were overdue. "And I'm Adilaah."

The name seemed to hang in the air like the note from an audacious Choir.

"Can I get you ladies a drink?" Nick offered politely as Fatima returned a stern expression. "Non-alcoholic of course."

"Why?" Adilaah shrugged playfully, allowing Nick to smile knowingly as he turned and walked back in the direction of the bar.

"I thought you wanted to get back!" Fatima declared sullenly.

"To what?" Adilaah retorted quickly, quashing her friend's protests.

"He's trouble," Fatima lamented further.

"That's why I like him," Adilaah countered lasciviously.

By the time Nick returned from the bar, Fatima had left and Adilaah had moved over to a decadent elevated glass version of a wooden gazebo, that partially hung off the roof, surrounded by a vista view of the Thames river. She gazed over it, watching the water irreverently lap onto the shore below from the reckless current. Grey clouds began to move in over the cityscape, permitting gleaming shards of amber light to filter through the water.

Nick moved in close to her as she turned to face him. He gently placed the Vodka and Cranberry Juice into her delicate hands almost as if he wanted to casually touch them.

"Where's your friend?" Nick inquired.

"She didn't want trouble," Adilaah answered suggestively, taking a small sip of the drink via the straw, and becoming overwhelmed by the sensation of alcohol.

"Like it?" Nick asked roguishly, "You've never had a drink before, have you?"

Adilaah widened her large brown eyes and stared into his, nodding truthfully. "Here…" Nick offered, attempting to take the poison away.

Adilaah pulled away rebelliously, "I want to," she declared petulantly taking large gulp of the drink. Her sudden defiance made her flippant and unknowingly sullen as a paltry reality settled over her previously vivacious inviting manner.

"You don't remember me," Nick proposed the question as he sensed her mood had changed. "Do you?"

"I do," Adilaah said contritely turning his back on him, "You're Ashraf's friend," speaking as though it was a subject that she preferred not to delve into. "The driver's son," She continued.

"I didn't think you would," Nick said with some relief.

"You were in the garden," Adilaah confirmed as the memory of their first meeting surfaced.

"You were in the window," Nick replied as he looked into her eyes, enchanted by her.

"They kept me locked away," she said dolefully, as she lowered her empty glass to the ground.

"Now you are free," Nick declared as he took her hand in his, releasing the glass and sending it crashing to the floor. He pulled her slowly toward him and she did little to resist. Softly and gently their lips met, as though they were waiting an eternity for them to touch. Their lips caressed as their mouths opened and with one breath took in each other's sacred essence. For a moment they were one, a complete being, beating from the same heart, thinking the same unitary thoughts. It was love consummate, holy, pure and glorious. For Nick, nothing in his life would ever be the same again. He was conjoined with an angel, and for one fleeting moment she allowed him, this mere mortal to experience the sanctity of immortality.

It was an epiphany.

That was how he remembered it.

7

The memory of his and Adilaah's first meeting still played like an unrequited anthem in Nick's mind. Amidst the conflict and clutter, their encounter seemed to resound through the essence of his being, and he felt spurned on to persevere in his solitary quest to find her murderer.

Nick barged through the doors to New Scotland Yard and wasted no time in making a hurried march for the basement to the Coroners laboratory. This time the place seemed brighter than before, despite being devoid of natural daylight. The recesses of the sterile white seemed to sparkle, benefitting from the freshly administered scrub that Aisha had been giving it.

Nick could tell that she was not in the mood for the interruption from visitors, not that she ever was. Aisha seemed to have a morbid attachment to the interior of the laboratory, as though the bleak cold steel surfaces and instruments seemed to harmonise with her personal demeanour. They demanded nothing of her flaccid character, only to be honoured in the ritual of sterilising and polishing. And she did this with a devotion that should have been meant for living things. But something told Nick that this was how she liked to maintain the status quo. Maintaining a subscription to a lifeless, underground existence where maintaining her ordered environment compensated for an internal chaotic struggle. The Met loved her for she was fantastic at her job and indeed many complex unsolvable cases met their end down here in this very lab, with Aisha putting her keen, albeit stifled intellect to work. Nick was hoping that this would be one of those occasions.

As Nick entered, Aisha had just completed scrubbing the main lab in the middle of the room, that didn't seem that dirty in the first place. Aisha proceeded to pick up her bucket of soapy suds and empty it into a sink as she noted Nick's entrance. She turned to face him, drying her hands vigorously and volunteering an uncomfortable smile at him. She motioned for him to take a seat at her desk and Nick accepted with a certain welcome relief. The fatigue was returning, and a large sigh erupted from his lungs as he sat down.

"You OK?" she inquired with an uncharacteristic kindness in her tone.

"Fine. You have something for me?" Nick replied with graciousness, grateful for her empathy.

"You asked me to keep this quiet, so I haven't put this on the reports. The compound traces we found in the victim's uterus was Opium," Aisha whispered under her breath.

"Opium? Why would she have Opium present in her Uterus?" Nick probed confused.

"Backdoor abortion," Aisha blurted with indignation. Nick stared at Aisha's revelation as it ignited a paralysing shock. A few moments passed as the words sank in.

"She was pregnant?" Nick lamented.

"It's common among Arabic women. Illegal abortions are conducted when a straw is tipped with Opium and it acts as an explosive, bursting the gestation sac and inducing a bleed out, "Aisha declared with deadpan efficiency. "Usually done in secret."

Nick remained silent as he considered the information.

"My guess is the pregnancy was unwanted," Aisha continued with a callous disregard that she was speaking about a real person.

"Thanks Aisha," Nick said genuinely. He now had a friend in the laboratory. "You did well," He continued, hoping that the gratitude would free some humanity from the mostly cold woman.

"And Nick," Aisha uttered as he rose to leave. "Taking into consideration who she was, tread carefully. There's usually a wall of silence around this stuff and they don't take politely to people asking questions."

Nick nodded as he realised Aisha's words were out of concern. He felt himself being swallowed deeper by this thing and suddenly he realised that his choices were taking him to places he did not really want to go. But only one thing seemed to remain – how he felt about Adilaah. And that kept him motivated.

~

The odour of decay had filled the place as though hope had been defeated and what remained was an air of despair. Nick walked down the corridor and peered into each of the rooms. Some women lay on decrepit beds, desperately staring at the mouldy warped ceiling, while others moved slowly through the corridor, blankly floating passed him like possessed ghosts, transfixed by tragedy. The Woman's Centre reeked of stagnancy; of lives stuck in limbo. They stared back at him with some repugnance making him feel like an intruder on their hallowed ground. They detested the fact that he was a man and that meant his action and very presence could not be trusted. He would not have been permitted inside, just as no other man would have been either, if he weren't a police detective.

He knew of this place. Adilaah mentioned it many times and during one of those times he actually paid attention to her noble and important efforts in helping these forsaken women. Many were destitute with nowhere else to go or no one to turn to. They were shunned and could not return to their families. Many had been turned out into the streets for defiling the protracted honour that they were meant to uphold. Some had fled abusive relationships, fed-up with being the punching bags of their husbands, fathers or brothers. Many had supposedly invited shame upon themselves and their families by being raped, while others had survived suicide attempts and now existed in a convoluted half-life between life and death. But these were only just some of the stories. Nick had known so many more. A life growing up in the inner city without a mother seemed to make these stories all the more prolific. He had tried to ignore them telling himself that ignorance was bliss, and that we all have our battles to fight. Compassion in the ghetto had always been an expensive luxury, especially when it was beyond the need for his own survival. That was how he felt until Adilaah came along. She had brought a ray of transmuting light that opened his cynical eyes and unforgiving heart. She had tried to make the plight of these woman easier, sharing a strange kindred spirit with them and giving of herself selflessly. She had the means to stay clear of this, and she often fought hard to ensure that she could descend from the ivory tower that she did not really belong to, and immerse herself in the disharmony and mayhem that was the human condition. And everywhere she went, and all those whom she had touched, she imparted an other-worldly love and compassion that she presided over them in a holy purity. Now that she was gone a very large vacant hole remained. Just the thought of it made Nick gloomy, that someone so pure could be whisked away so violently. That she was rewarded for her generosity of spirit with such wretched indignity.

Nick saw Fatima as she spoke to one of her colleagues. Fatima was barely recognisable to him, compared with the glamorous, pristine and polished woman that he remembered perched on the end of a designer sun lounger by that rooftop pool. She looked older, almost haggard and aged with blotchy skin, rank flat grey flecked hair concealed in a pale head scarf. As Nick confronted her she apprehensively tried to avoid his gaze and reacted almost like she sought a quick exit.

"What do you want here?" Fatima enquired antagonistically.

"I need to ask you some questions," Nick asserted with ardent authority.

"I have nothing to say to you Nick," she retorted. "You shouldn't even be in here. Please just go."

"It's to do with Adilaah," Nick reasoned, hoping she would want to help him in his quest.

"Look Adilaah is gone and I'm not going to disgrace her memory by being seen talking to you of all people."

"Adilaah was pregnant," Nick announced. "Did you know about that?"

Fatima brazenly looked around to see if anybody had heard Nick's utterance.

"Let's go in here," She ushered, quickly moving Nick in to the privacy of a nearby office, closing the door behind her.

Fatima moved in closer to Nick, rubbing her forehead and tired eyes preparing herself for the difficult words she was about to speak.

"I don't believe I am telling you this."

"Fatima, just tell me," Nick encouraged, eager to get to the bottom of the issue.

Fatima was silent for a moment.

"She came to me a few months ago," Fatima spoke. "She was desperate and didn't want anyone to find out especially her father."

"Do you think they found out?" Nick probed inquisitively.

"I don't know," Fatima said dourly.

"Did she tell you who the father was?" Nick asked tentatively.

Fatima shook her head grimly trying to avoid the course of Nick's questioning.

"Don't lie to me," Nick bellowed at the Fatima's evasion of the truth.

"Kusam Nick," Fatima pleaded. "She wanted to protect me, so she didn't tell me."

"Go on," Nick encouraged.

"I took her to see this woman who arranged it back in Lahore. Told her father she was visiting cousins and had it done," Fatima replied despondently, sitting down as she spoke. "I didn't see her much after that. She was never the same again."

"When did you see her last?" Nick questioned blankly.

"A few of months ago. She seemed different."

"Different. How?" Nick inquired further.

"I don't know!" Fatima declared loudly, "She will take her secrets to the grave," Fatima looked up accusingly at Nick. "Like everything in her life."

"I can't let her go like that," Nick said with purpose. "Without the justice she deserves…"

"Justice. Look around you at all these women, battered, abandoned, raped. Where's their justice?" Fatima scoffed as she stood up with determination and pulled her plain Headscarf aside, revealing the blotchy scarred skin on her neck and shoulder.

"This is the only justice I know. Thanks to my father – he found out that I was friends with an English boy. He had acid thrown on me. Said I brought shame on him. How do think I ended up here?" Fatima bellowed as the pain of her injuries released tears from her otherwise guarded composure.

"Adilaah was the only one I could turn to," Fatima continued, "And in the end I failed her."

Fatima retreated into her seat, covered up her scars and placed her head in her hands, slowly wiping the tears away from her weary eyes.

"We both did," Nick said dejected, as he placed a comforting hand on Fatima's back.

"She knew what she as up against, and she couldn't run away from it," Fatima said regaining her composure. "Not even for you."

Fatima stood up once more to leave but stopped and looked Nick squarely in the eye.

"Even though she really wanted to."

She spoke with conviction so that he would not misinterpret her words.

8

The ceiling to his flat was sprawled out like a canvas as the events of the day played out in an imaginary kaleidoscope above Nick, as he lay face up in his bed. Fatigue had overtaken any normal function and sleep would have been a welcome antidote, but the thoughts of Adilaah abated any restful seclusion. He could see her in all the memories that seemed as though they were fresh from a few days before. All the emotions and heartbreak that he assumed he had vanquished, suddenly reared their intrusive heads and tormented his soul.

In frustration he rolled around in his bed facing the empty pillow beside him. Then suddenly and as if by some magical alchemy she was beside him. Her chamois powder smooth skin, delicate small perfectly formed nose, striding above a pair of full pout ruby red lips. Her face was in perfect symmetry, formed by a sacred geometry that was complemented by large round brown eyes that seemed to reach deep into one's soul and find the good in it. It was impossible not to fall in love with her. She had something that everybody sought – an ability to make everything she touched beautiful, and by that touch, she could ensue pure poetry. Nick closed his eyes and he was transported back to a time when she was in his bed.

~

Adilaah laid on the bed dressed in an elegant pastel blue blouse and tailored trouser. She had kicked her high heeled court shoes off and curled up in comfort-able foetal position with her arms together, coupled under her cheek. She lay in front of Nick, as he extended his right hand and caressed her face gently, Adilaah took serene delight in the soothing gesture, taking hold of it and coupling it with her own hands under her cheek.

Nick sensed Adilaah's anxiousness as she took his hand and clasped it under hers. It was more than an affectionate gesture. He could feel her pulse quicken and the palm of her hands were moist with the sweat of trepidation. Nick placed his other hand on her thigh and again he felt her clench her resolve, prompting him to move in closer and reassuringly place a gentle kiss on her soft lips. Adilaah clasped his hand tighter and inhaled deeply, drawing in all of Nick's essence. He felt her consume him, and all of his doubt, susceptibility and weakness was drawn out by some spell that she had cast from her lips and her bewitching form. For a moment he wondered how someone who could command such power over his emotions, feel so anxious by his touch. But he could feel her anxiety fading as the kiss pervaded and he felt the overwhelming compulsion to touch every part of her delectable body. In the moment, the inexorable passion of the embrace engulfed his senses and he tightened his hand on her soft thighs, and gently moved it up, following her curvaceous form until he could feel the sensation of her bare waist under her blouse. The intrusion of his hand on her skin without the barrier of clothing made her tense and turn onto her back. She still clung onto his right hand like it was an anchor rooted in reality, but she left his other hand where it was, laying firmly across her stomach, flat and spread over her belly-button.

Afternoon sunlight peeked through the closed curtains and evoked mirrored patterns across the bed like wild shards of dancing glass. Nick gazed at them, mesmerised by the patterns on Adillaah's shapely figure. A patent energy electrified him and travelled throughout his body, via his frozen hand, transmitting through to Adilaah's midriff. She could feel the intensity of anticipation between them, like a palpable tension that opponents felt in a chess game, each trying to out strategize each other, but relishing the riveting exchange. Carefully, almost as if he did not want to disturb the exchange, he moved his fingers over her trembling skin. The caress was more powerful than any orgasm, a scintillation overload that made her belly retract as she inhaled deeply. Gently he unbuttoned the lowest button and with the movement of a snail approached the next. She watched this hand while still grasping the other, moving her eyes provocatively to meet his. Nick smiled reassuringly, fostering trust in his wandering exploits. He undid the next button, slowly parting the blouse like a stage curtain. Her breathing quickened and so did his as he exposed most of her waist to the low-lit bedroom. Nick lowered his head over her stomach and kissed her belly button. She tasted of creamy vanilla and sweet musk. Her skin had become moist and silky from the fragrant sweat of exhilaration. He licked her glowing skin with the end of his pointed tongue and kissed it lightly.

Then he looked at the final hurdle. The blouse still masked her ample breasts, marked by the small indents that were made by her erect nipples. She looked back at him as her eyes permitted him to proceed. Nick unbuttoned the last fixture and gently unveiled her pert bosom. They sat comfortably and full inside a low-cut ivory coloured silk bra that just about covered her milk chocolate nipples. Nick pressed his eager lips between them. The impression of his lips made her quiver, as she rigidly pointed her legs and curled toes. He then kissed her gently on the lips, sucking each one and then coaxing her tongue from its refuge. Finally, he brought his hand up to the bra and with no fuss unclipped the front-clasp. Her bosom emerged into freedom and the exposure of her intimate body to Nick's entranced eyes seemed ecstatic and terrifying all at the same time. Nick could see her wrestling with the compulsion to want to cover up, but the unthreatening look in his eyes made her resist and she lay before him exposed like she never had been before. Perhaps Adilaah saw something that she never saw before, and that was love. Love that inspired trust that the person before you only intended the best for you, and while exposing her body may have been new to her, she felt safe knowing that he would tenderly embrace her in the way that she deserved.

They both felt it – an unspoken trust and security that was borne out of a higher experience, one that was holy and pure. One that had perhaps spanned the ages. He felt as though she would trust him with anything, without condition, almost as if she had placed her entire life in his hands. A part of him shuddered at the responsibility and immense implications, for it did not seem routed in any form of reality. But at that moment he didn't care. This gift was in his arms and he felt like he had finally caught a break and the gods had smiled on him with this abundant reward, and there was no way he was going to second guess it. He kissed Adilaah again like she needed his life-giving spirit and he revelled in the sanctity of the moment. He kissed her neck and then her chest. Her skin tasted of revitalising nectar, and he licked it like it was honey, moving slowly towards her breasts. Adilaah held her breath in anticipation of his mouth on her breasts. She clasped his right hand even tighter and then placed her other on his head as he enticed her plump left bosom. Nick tickled the areola of her hard nipples and then placed his entire mouth over the nub and pulled on them, tantalising her with pleasure. Adilaah moaned slightly, cocking her neck back on the pillow, as Nick moved over to her other breast. Adilaah had become hot from the excitement and this only spurred his efforts. She gripped his hair tightly, but Nick persisted, as her excitement reached a fever pitch. He, himself had become overwhelmed with pleasure and felt the erect pressure build in his jeans. His breathing quickened as he pressed up against the side of her bottom and crossed his left leg over hers. He wanted to rip everything off of her and behold this Persian beauty with unreserved passion. He wanted to hold her in a way that she would understand how he truly felt, how he had always felt. He wanted them to experience a union that defied separation and embraced each other as though they were one being. He moved his hand down along her stomach and under her trouser. He found the edge of her silk panty and threw caution to the wind. He slipped his hand triumphantly over the wet bulbous mounds between her legs, further sinking his middle finger into the slippery flesh. He felt exuberated and a wet fluid filled his underpants.

But just as she granted permission to touch her cherished inner most aspects, she withdrew it. Suddenly, she closed her legs with a steadfast grip and yanked his offending hand from her trouser. And with the same resolve that the pleasure entered, it exited. Adilaah recoiled and withdrew her permissiveness. Suddenly that reality had come rushing back and the purity of their lovemaking had no place in it. Adilaah covered her breasts and then curled up in a cocoon, rolling away from Nick. He could not understand what he had done wrong. Adilaah's expression had gone from one of exuberance to bleakness, and she detached from the connection that they had just shared. All of a sudden, she was distant, and Nick could sense that she was a different person, as if some sort of failsafe had unwittingly kicked in.

"What's wrong?" Nick inquired tenderly.

"This," Adilaah retorted coldly, staring blankly into space, then without cordiality sat up abruptly, got to her feet and declared, "I should go." Nick watched her as she sullenly got dressed.

"Have I done something?" Nick asked.

"No," Adilaah replied bluntly, reconstituting her hair and make-up.

"Is it so hard?" Nick ventured, "To just be yourself and answer to no one."

"You don't understand," Adilaah replied with a cracked voice as tears fill her eyes and she tried to mouth words that wouldn't come. Nick moved up to her, kneeling on the bed and placed his arms around her waist.

"Then make me," Nick said convincingly, pulling her closer, "I…"

"Don't…don't say it," Adilaah exclaimed quickly, feeling Nick's emotion enrapturing her own.

"But I want to," Nick offered as he felt Adilaah's resolve weaken.

"It will just complicate things," She said dourly.

"That is what we are…" Nick affirmed despondently. "Unspoken words."

~

Nick could still hear the words he spoke at Adilaah in that very room when the shrill sound of the electronic buzzer disturbed his reflection. He reluctantly dragged his exhausted body from his unmade bed and plodded through his small flat through the short hallway and into the living-cum-dining room straddled by a sleek and compact modern kitchen.

The sun had quit for the day and the laminate floor possessed an inhospitable coldness as he stepped over it in his woollen socks. He rubbed his shirtless slim muscular upper body as he lifted the receiver off of the intercom saddle.

"Yeah?" he barked disinterested in the voice that belonged to his interruption.

"It's me! Let me up," Came the impatient bilious reply. He knew all too well who the voice belonged to, and he was in no shape to deal with her outspoken antics tonight. But he knew that she would continue to pester the button to the entrance door, until he would have no choice but to let her up. Thereafter would follow the run-of-the-mill tussle before he would succumb to her wayward charms and she would end up staying with him knowing full well that he preferred the warmth of her robust body compared with the cold emptiness of nobody. Nick pressed the button on the intercom and the front door released.

It was a few moments before the rapturous plod of Carley's footsteps could be heard stomping up the stairs. Nick unlocked the door and turned the door knob allowing the door to slide open of its own accord in preparation for his guest. Nick stood ready for Carley's appearance as he caressed the cold bare skin on his chest and rubbed the tiredness from his eyes. As they refocused, there she stood. The door to his flat creaked open to reveal her casually leaning against the door frame. She took his appearance in – bare feet, unbuckled denim jeans and bare chested, rounded off with a temperate scowl in response to her intrusion. She raised her eyebrows and said, "Ready for me then."

Carley slammed the door, announcing her arrival with fervour. She strolled in and unhooked the thick strap from broad shoulders, dropping the fully loaded bag onto the floor. With equal zest, she slid off her studded patent leather jacket and kicked off her shoes. Nick watched her as she seemed to settle in without much need for permission, almost as if she was returning to the marital home after a long day at work. Today she looked surprisingly coordinated, which left Nick with a feeling of adoration. She fashioned a fitted all-black cocktail dress, which on its own seemed to suggest a decency in her manner. Nevertheless, it was still short enough to land just below her rear and snug enough to reveal that she was sporting no underwear. So much for decency. But somehow Nick seemed to like it. In truth he always did, and she knew it. For all he knew there was a side to her that curled up in bed with soft pink pyjamas and furry bunny slippers every night, but that was a side that he had never seen, and never wanted to.

Carley knelt down and rummaged around in her overflowing bag to produce an opened bottle of Jack Daniels. Then she stood proudly, holding it aloft as if she were a spokesmodel, displaying a slight sway in her stance that only an intoxicated person would embody.

"Peace offering," Carley offered amiably.

"You've had some," Nick said, noting her slurring offer.

"You were off the cranberry juice," Carley retorted, "So I thought you might be in the mood for something stronger." She closed in on him, slowly uncapping the bottle and stopping before him. She lifted the bottle to her pouting pink lips and took an unceremonious swig of the bourbon, swallowing as it crucified her throat on the way down. She placed her free hand on his chest, stroked his pecks, ruffling his black chest hair, then moved up to the back of his neck. Then she took another generous swig of the alcohol and planted her lips on his and injected the saliva mixed liquor down his throat.

Nick should have spat the liquid out and kicked the temptress out, but the coaxing of her rich and over-powering body musk combined with her bewitching allure, seemed to override any sense of resistance that he had in him. He swallowed the liquid fire down, lubricated with honeyed saliva and the taste of a lascivious tongue. Then with a vigour that resembled domination, she retracted her mouth and rested the bottle on the floor. She stood erect just as quickly and attacked his lips with voracious intent, seemingly hungry enough to bite them on occasion. Nick could feel an insatiable passion rise from a hidden recess. It was uncontrollable, animalistic and undeniable. She didn't kiss him, she possessed him and there was nothing he could do to stop her once she got going. Most men would give anything to have a woman like Carley in their lives, to be worshipped with a carnal instinct and make love like she was wading into battle – relentless and unwavering. He realised, as she devoured his neck and ears like an overfraught beast, that this unbridled passion had its root in some form of raw affection, and that is why he had made the sacrifices for her, risking his career and morality. Deep down she provided him with some sort of tangible survival, in exchange for the life he in turn liberated her from. Maybe it was a morbid love. He wasn't sure.

Carley pushed Nick back onto his brown upholstered sofa and pulled him lower down by his knees. She positioned herself between his legs, leaning over and clawing at his chest, from the shoulder slowly down through to quivering stomach. Nick felt his pulse race as she stroked his belly, then she hooked her hands firmly under his jeans and yanked them down sharply, liberating his swollen penis. Nick's heart pumped like an Olympic sprinter as Carley eyed his throbbing manhood, teasingly gazing at it. She grabbed the base of it and tighten her grasp over it, ensuring it was as hard as it could be. Then she peeled back the foreskin of his partially peaking hood and caressed it with her small tongue. She watched his face as she toyed with his tip, giving it successive licks as she did. She could tell he wanted her to swallow all of it, and she smirked cheekily as she gobbled the entire thing all the way down her throat.

Carley spent a few minutes massaging Nick's penis with her rampant tongue, getting him as ready as she could without squandering her efforts all too prematurely. She elegantly rose to her feet and removed her dress over her head, tossing it onto the floor, revealing her naked body. Nick studied her athletic curves that started with broad shoulders, propped up by her remarkably upright posture. Her straight back and neck allowed her pert ample breasts to stand to attention. They were so firm and upright that they could have been mistaken for being fake, something Carley vehemently denied, but Nick did not really care. Her prominent breasts sat proudly over a small waist that bore a small tummy, a rounded milky white bum and a neat, elegant slit that rose perfectly from between her legs. From the front her smooth porcelain vagina was barely visible until she spread her muscular legs or when she bent over, revealing a sculpted mound, closely flanked by her plump cheeks.

Carley knelt over Nick's body resting her knees on the sofa and lining his penis for her wet vagina. Nick gave her full control as she yanked his stiff manhood and inserted into her moist passage. She saddled her weight along her knees and brought her all of her body over his, taking his entire length inside her. Carley wasted no time in thrashing up and down, riding the contour of his penis while using her fingers to invigorate her swelling clitoris. The sweet electric jolts of ecstasy enjoyed by the stimulation of her fingers, motivated her to work harder and faster.

Nick felt the throbbing excitement of his penis reach climax and he lifted his hands to massage Carley's breasts, but she revolted, slapping them back and pinning them under her knees.

"Don't cum yet," She exclaimed as she began to move up and down with increased frequency and vigour, her entire body tensing into excruciating contortions of pleasure. She rubbed her clitoris even harder and began to shriek with the vocal range of a seasoned operatic tenor. Nick did his best to hold onto his load as the undeniable pressure began to arise from the base of his scrotum. Although he could feel the inside of Carley's pussy tighten almost as if she was trying to expel him while milking him at the same time. She slowly began to settle into a shallow waddle, reverberating as if she was on a rodeo bronco, and then she pushed one more time at the bud above her flaps and she froze her entire body as the ominous joy of a full orgasm enveloped her completely. A loud shriek turned into a whimper, as Nick could feel the wall of her vagina expand and then release a small squirt of warm liquid. Her head fell as she bent double over him. Then she kissed him firmly on the lips and dis-mounted, dropping back down to her knees onto the floor between his. She could see the expectation that had built up in his face. He needed release. She filled her mouth with his quaking penis and sucked onto it a few times, before caressing the hood with her tongue. Nick quivered uncontrollably as his buttocks tightened, and Carley gripped both cheeks of his butt with her strong hands, pulling his dick into the back of her throat. That was all it took as he ejaculated his full load into her willing mouth. Then when he was done she plopped down on the sofa next to him and they lay together uninhibited, finally at peace with each other.

9

Nick's eyes opened to the invading daylight that steaked into the dark apartment. He could not remember a time when he had slept so soundly and the fatigue he had so bravely fought, seemed to have abated. He rubbed some clarity into his eyes as the white stippled ceiling came into stark focus. Under the satin duvet Carley's heavy arm lay straddled across his waist. His eyes shifted over to her cocooned form snuggled tightly in the bed linen with only the hint of a forehead and unruly blonde hair. He carefully moved her arm off himself and slid out from under the duvet, slipping on his carelessly discarded denim jeans and throwing on a t-shirt that had a picture of Guns n' Roses across the front.

Nick pushed open the drapes of the living room with conviction, scanning the small Victorian square which lay in front of his building. It was enclosed by a decorative black steel fence and dotted with old Oak amidst well-tendered gardens. He took pleasure in staring out of his flat window into those gardens, studying the local inhabitants going about their day –

joggers keeping up their healthy regime, whizzing past older folk who had lived in that part of Camden long before the 'money' moved in, along with anxious mothers barely containing precocious mischievous toddlers, wishing they had never given up independence for motherhood.

The scene brought Nick a moment of serenity that made him grateful for his achievements, despite it not coming without a degree of struggle. Somehow this simple scape put things in perspective and he realised how far he had come, clawing his way out of London's concrete tower block slums and escaping into this idyllic middle-class sanctuary.

Nick basked in the glow of the morning sun, almost meditating to its magnificence. Then a hand came down over his neck and slid down the contour of his back. A foreboding kiss on his unprepared lips followed leaving him little chance for resistance.

"Good morning," She declared looking nothing like the vixen that took advantage of his body the previous night. This morning she looked fulfilled and blissful, almost as if the beast was still asleep and this congruous version was sent forth. Carley looked radiant, with none of the latent effects of hard liquor. She looked vivacious and bubbly as though she had woken from a sleepover wearing one of Nick's rock themed t-shirts, stretching it over her private parts as she plonked down on the sofa that was the setting to the previous night's erotic escapade.

Nick stared at her profusely, as though he suddenly belonged to a bizarre alternate reality. Was he still dreaming? Surely this wasn't the Carley Banks he knew? But there she sat, like an overhyped teen with a false sense of adolescent security. No scorn or scowl, pithy retorts or overconfidence masking a deep seated inferiority complex. Whatever this side was, he had not seen it before. It took him by surprise to realise that she was even capable of such polite behaviour, and that garnered an underlying reaction of adoration and generosity toward her. He felt his defensiveness dissolve, realising that there was now this side to her, a side which could garner trust.

"What are you up to today?" She enquired gleefully.

"Work probably," Nick declared flatly, as he came to terms with this new caring side of Carley.

"Oh," Carley responded with disappointment. "But you've been working so hard all week. Couldn't you take a day off?"

Nick gazed at her as she spoke, realising that she sounded increasingly like a neglected girlfriend, rather than the matter-of-fact emotionally stunted individual that he had gotten used to. And a part of him cowered with trepidation at this display of vulnerability.

"My first case and I need to impress," he replied trying to garner empathy.

"Oh, and what case would that be?" she retorted as the scorn returned.

"The Khan murder," Nick replied.

"The one in the news?" Carley questioned bluntly as the vulnerability in her voice ebbed away. "Detective and high-flying murder case all in one week!" She scoffed.

Nick's affection turned back to disdain, as he deflated, exhaling deeply and shutting his eyes in frustration.

"Nevertheless…" Nick reasoned. "She needs me."

"She needs you?" Carley bellowed. "Why would she need you?"

"She needs her murderer to be brought to justice," Nick declared emphatically.

Carley turned away from him, shaking her head gravely.

"You just don't get it do you?" Carley lamented with venom. "Ron, McNeill, this case. It's all been set up so that they can get what they want…"

"And what's that?" Nick barked loudly.

"I don't know," Carley resounded. "But I know who'll be left with nothing in the end – You!"

Carley leapt to her feet heading toward the bedroom, just as Nick grabbed her hand preventing her from leaving.

"Stay," Nick said with an impassioned voice.

"What for?" Carley responded with contempt,

latching her hand from his and storming off into the bedroom.

Carley had gathered up her things and left without a word or shudder of emotion. It hadn't taken long before things spiralled back to where they always were. Nick knew that he could not dilute his quest to find Adilaah's killer, a mission that resonated deep down and he felt the overwhelming need to persist. He could not bring himself to tell Carley that he was investigating the murder of an ex-lover, who still haunted him to this day. He knew that Carley wouldn't be so receptive to that and that she would need a few days to simmer down, before she would be back. She always came back. Besides, where else could she go? Nevertheless, he felt a slight remorse at how things had been left, especially as the morning had begun so amiably. A part of him felt a new connection with this side of Carley – susceptible and gracious, but he didn't want to get his hopes up.

The mechanical ringtone from his mobile phone interrupted his thought patterns, and as he reached out for it. He noted the private number.

"D-C Shankar," Nick answered in an authoritative voice.

"Shank?" The muffled voice questioned.

"Yes?" Nick replied confused as nobody had called him that name in years.

"It's Ashraf. Ashraf Khan," The voice replied confidently.

"Not someone I was expecting Ashraf," Nick confirmed with surprise.

"I know." Ashraf answered despondently, "Can we meet?"

"Err..." Nick dithered, unsure whether to accept.

"I've got something. It's to do with Adilaah," Ashraf stuttered.

Nick remained silent for a moment to consider his options. He wasn't sure how to process this.

Why did Ashraf choose to come to him? What did he have on Adilaah? Did he somehow know about their love affair? Worse still, did he know about her pregnancy and assume that he was the father?

"Where?" Nick said tentatively as the questions raced through his mind.

"Stratford. Boxing Gym on the High street. About three? Come alone," Ashraf instructed bluntly and hung up the phone. Nick lingered over the call, cradling his phone. This call from Ashraf was odd. They had not spoken in years and when they last did, it was not cordial. A sinking feeling churned inside him, and Carley's words began to echo – *you'll be left with nothing in the end.*

~

Nick sat slouched in in his office chair, reclining behind his dishevelled desk. It was a Saturday and the office was deserted, with the rows of desks eerily quiet. He stared engrossed at the computer screen before him, the index finger of his right hand carefully pressing the arrow key on the keyboard. The other hand cradled an extra-large coffee cup with the words Starbucks branded on it. Nick sipped the hot Americano, swallowing a few gulps before returning to the detail on the screen. The screen displayed an arrest mug-shot of Ashraf Khan. Nick studied the picture as Ashraf's ill-natured eyes stared back. They seemed to stir something unnatural in Nick's gut, that inflamed a sense of discord. That feeling took him back to that day.

"You Paki's need to stay away from this park!" The one with wavy blonde hair shouted. At first Nick could not even understand what he was saying. He had quite naively thought that the boy was making some kind of joke. Perhaps they were just 'avin a laaff' as he'd hear them always say but didn't quite know what it meant. His father always taught him to speak properly – the Queen's English he called it. "When I drove the Ambassador around, that is what he expected, and nothing less!" Rohit always reminisced over his service as a driver for the first British Ambassador to newly independent India. At age eleven, Nick had heard it so many times that he stopped listening. But when he got to the stories of Nick's mother then he paid attention. Nick did not know that much about her. He knew from his father's whisky-laden anecdotes that she was the Ambassador's daughter, a much younger, free-spirited rebel; Ethel would do the opposite of everything that her father expected from her or from any self-respecting English girl for that matter. It was love at first sight his father always declared proudly, and they would steal her father's car and sneak off to the various Delhi hide outs and christen the fine leather seats. That's probably where Nick was conceived, because after the many torrid backseat exploits she became pregnant. And unwilling to brave the scandal and shame that would ensue from the affair between a 'Coolie' and a promiscuous high society English rose, they eloped to Kenya to live on her sister's tea estate. And that's where Nick would have grown up. Perhaps as a spoilt disillusioned half-breed outcast not quite sure where his true roots lay. But her spirit and appetite for other partners was more than Rohit could manage nor bare. Ethel was his reckless abandonment in an otherwise mediocre and steady life, and for that he was now saddled with a lifelong reminder of that escapade. It was not long that their opposing cultural, social and personal ambitions began to polarize their self-worth and Rohit decided that he would come to England, along with his three-year old son, to find the placid safe life that he was more suited to, leaving Ethel to continue the life of excess and exuberance.

Ashraf had heard the boy's slur clearly, and he wasn't prepared to let this go. Ashraf marched up to the boy who was probably about fourteen or fifteen, Nick had guessed, as he followed behind Ashraf nervously.

The bully stood tall and forbearing as Ashraf confronted him.

"I didn't catch that from all the way over there," Ashraf said with undue confidence.

"I said keep out of this park! You don't belong here," The boy announced, almost spitting on Ashraf's face who seemed unnervingly calm.

"You called us something else," Ashraf probed, listening intently for the reply.

"Paki is what I said," The bully lamented.

"Were you talking about him or me?" Ashraf continued.

A small crowd of kids had gathered around the scene of this unusual altercation. Nick began to close in on Ashraf sensing that he had a plan for this bully, his nervousness turning into a resolute confidence.

"Both of you!" The bully screeched.

"Well this is my friend Nick," Ashraf jested, "We call him Nick because he is only half Indian. Other half English."

Ashraf put his arm around Nick and ushered him forward so that they both stood in front of this much taller Cretan who, hadn't anticipated this partisan exchange to ensue from his callous outburst. Nick stared at the boy with anxiousness.

"You were wrong to call him a Paki you see,"

Ashraf affirmed, "No I am from Pakistan. Well my father is. I was born here in Britain. We own that big house up there."

Ashraf pointed at the large mansion not far from the park.

"Do you see it?" Ashraf asked as he smiled courteously.

The boy avoided looking as Ashraf seemed to have gained the upper hand in the standoff, with the boy's position looking far weaker now.

"We have a right to walk through this park. Show me your house. Is it near?" Ashraf questioned as he looked around. But the boy remained silent, his eminence draining.

"Not here is it?" Ashraf inquired as his face had become choleric, "Where are you from?"

"Finchley," The boy stammered.

"Finchley," Ashraf considered, slowly nodding. Ashraf looked at his crowd of spectators and then back at the bully with a smirk. Then as if he had been possessed by a demonic power, Ashraf curled up his fist and swung it at the boy's jaw, careening across it with a crunch. The boy dropped like lifeless sack of potatoes. The crowd of kids who had gathered, scattered, including those who had accompanied this loudmouth, who by now was a curled-up lump on the ground. Nick himself backed away at the speed at which Ashraf had levelled this boy. He watched as Ashraf stood over boy with a vicious malevolent smirk. Nick realised that his best friend had an unpredictable violent streak that he never wanted to be on the wrong side of. He kept his distance while he watched Ashraf circle his victim.

"You're the one who doesn't belong here Finchley," Ashraf bellowed as he kicked the boy once more in the stomach and marched off. Nick faithfully followed.

As if Nick's memory of Ashraf's onslaught on the bully wasn't enough, the sudden appearance of Ron Allen at his desk made Nick feel even more apprehensive. He hadn't seen Ron since the Hearing, and he had been avoiding the confrontation that an interaction with Ron would inevitably bring.

Ron stood bearing down on Nick making his lofty presence felt. He was a looming, hulk of a man with an aggressive obtrusive manner that discounted everybody else's. If there was an archetype for the type of overbearing, intimidating, loutish officer, then Ron would fit it perfectly, and there was a very thin line between the job of detective and career criminal, which he seemed to straddle rather carelessly between. Nick did not enjoy spending time or engaging with the man, but his career meant he had to call Ron partner and so he succumbed begrudgingly. There was a big part of him that relished the idea that McNeill had asked him to follow this investigation discreetly and on his own. If Ron were involved it would have been anything but discreet, for as McNeill had told him, Ron was too much of a blunt instrument.

"Haven't seen you around. You avoiding me?" Ron jested as he scouted the paperwork on the desk and Ashraf's image on the computer screen.

"No mate," Nick replied as he closed the paperwork file on the desk and minimized the file on the computer screen.

Ron pulled a chair from the neighbouring desk and slumped down on it, making his intrusion felt even more.

"So, I heard you were reassigned. McNeil's thrown you a big juicy one to get your teeth into. Seems the reward can be large for Detectives with the right skills. And you seem to have all the right skills," Ron waxed.

"Skills?" Nick scoffed.

"I risked everything for you because of that little stunt you pulled with Tyson," Nick exclaimed, facing up to Ron. Nick's words managed to deflate Ron's incendiary tone.

"Munroe been to see you?" Ron quizzed.

"No," Nick replied solemnly.

"Don't fucking lie to me. I've noticed the two of you and your little chats. You'd better keep your mouth shut, if you know what's good for you!" Ron threatened, leaning in toward Nick.

"I know how to handle Miles," Nick reassured.

"You better!" Ron barked furtively, "You are just as guilty as I am, and I won't go down alone."

Ron pushed the chair back forcefully as he stood up, glaring at Nick as he walked off.

10

The doorway to the gym was unassuming, and Nick could have easily missed it. The entrance consisted of an aluminium glass door that had streaks of dirt from the street. Nick pushed the decrepit door, which screeched open, grinding as it scored the green vinyl floor. He stepped through slowly and released the door. It slammed with a loud wallop drowning out the roar of the high street car and bus traffic. A long gloomy staircase led upward from the doorway. Nick summed up his courage and took a deep breath as he ascended the staircase unsure of what awaited him at the end of it. He had not checked in his position or logged the phone call like he should have. He did not know what to make of the phone call from Ashraf or the apparent information that he had for him.

Had something changed between them? Was Ashraf prepared to forget the past and make amends? Had Adilaah's death made him realise certain truths?

These questions permeated Nick's thoughts as he ascended the flight of stairs, eventually reaching the top and arriving into a large roof space that was dominated by a large boxing ring in the middle. Nick carefully paced his way through the myriad of red and blue floor mats, squat benches and weights, along a path that led toward the centre ring. Nick watched as one of the fighters, a young Afro-Caribbean man rhythmically pounded on a Speed bag and seemed to jab harder as he studied Nick. Not far away another trainee fighter thumped at a heavy hanging punching bag, each strike delivered with a ferociousness that stemmed from a pent-up rage.

Nick could feel the entire building super-charged with a fury-laden venom, coupled with a dry and dank combination of sweat and bleach. He felt the distinctive preponderance of distrust and disharmony which left him unsettled, almost as if they could smell he was a detective and made that him immediately unwelcome. Ashraf had seen him as he first entered but shifted his attention back toward the two sparring fighters, circling each other in the ring. Nick walked up to Ashraf with determination, eager to get this encounter over and done with.

Ashraf extended his hand as Nick approached. Nick stared at it, as the gesture took him by surprise. He reluctantly shook it sensing Ashraf was just as nervous as he was, as their sweaty palms locked together. Nick's keen eye noticed a sparkling gold Moon and Star emblem on a chain around Ashraf's wrist.

"Thanks for coming," Ashraf said cordially as he retracted his hand.

"No problem," Nick replied as he sensed a friendlier tone in Ashraf's voice that belonged to the friend he once knew. "So, you train fighters here?"

"Yes. My cousin's training for the Welterweight title," Ashraf answered.

"Any good?" Nick ventured.

"See for you yourself. He's the one in blue." Ashraf said and pointed at the more dominated fighter in the ring. Nick then turned his attention to the boxer decked in blue shorts and gloves. To Nick, he seemed more agile and quicker on the attack, moving around the ring with more speed and virility. That was the depth of Nick's assessment of the boxer with his limited knowledge of the sport.

"Do you remember when we would play fight in my room?" Ashraf recollected gleefully.

"Didn't feel like playing to me!" Nick laughed. "And besides, you always won."

"You always dropped your guard," Ashraf replied. "That's when I struck."

Nick smiled politely at Ashraf, whose words seemed far more loaded than perhaps he had intended. He always felt that Ashraf had perceived him weaker when they were boys, almost as if he had wanted to protect his best friend. But somehow Nick felt that Ashraf gained some kind of gratitude from it, as though Ashraf revelled in it and that was the only reason they had been friends, so that he could dominate Nick and make him feel inferior.

Indeed, Nick was the only person with whom Ashraf could be superior with, for everybody else had made him feel inferior. His father seemed to have a possessive love for his favourite, and that was Adilaah, with little emotion to spare for his son. Nick had known nothing of Ashraf's mother, what happened to her, and the subject was never brought up. And even the many servants seemed to treat him with an irreverent disregard stemming from the knowledge that if his father didn't really care then why should they. Nick was his only remorseful ally, and that is why Ashraf latched onto him so strongly, for he was the only one who had shown Ashraf any affection and devotion, despite the fact that Ashraf took every advantage to exploit and abuse his vulnerabilities.

Ashraf had led Nick into an office at the rear of the gym that sported a large window which oversaw the entire space.

"You know I want to help in any way I can," Ashraf said as he closed the door to the office.

Nick nodded slowly, unsure of where Ashraf was going with this.

"We found Adilaah's killer," Ashraf declared.

Nick gazed back at Ashraf, perplexed and

shocked, as he spoke, "What are you talking about?"

"The flat where Adilaah's body was found, belonged to an Iraqi family who allowed a man named Nadir Suleiman to live there. He's a Kurdish refugee," Ashraf carefully pointed out.

"How did you find this out?" Nick enquired, unsure of how to process this revelation.

"A witness," Ashraf said. "He saw this man with my sister. When he learned who Adilaah was, he came forward."

"Who is he? I need to question him," Nick said resolutely.

"He won't talk to the police. Just us," Ashraf advised.

"I need a signed deposition…" Nick uttered, but Ashraf was quick to intervene.

"We took care of everything," he said as he held a brown envelope in front of Nick. "Like I said we would."

Nick tentatively took a hold of it and removed a photograph of Nadir Suleiman. Instantly the contours of the man's face brought recognition into Nicks mind. This was the same man whom he glimpsed in the crowd at the scene of the crime, who seemed to be particularly invested in him.

More glossy photographs occupied the contents of the envelope and Nick removed them. He studied them carefully as each one harboured another sordid revelation. The first pictured

Adilaah and Nadir in each other's arms, then next showed them in passionate embrace. Nick shuffled hastily through them as each photograph prompted anguished jealousy, causing a subdued rage to well up within.

"You were having her followed?" Nick asked as he looked up at Ashraf.

"My father felt it was for her own good," Ashraf replied convincingly. "And as it turns out, he was right."

"They were romantically involved…" Nick voiced disconcerted.

Ashraf was silent for a moment, staring at Nick as he considered his reply. "Adilaah didn't always do as she was told."

"I suppose not," Nick retorted, replacing the photographs into the envelope.

"Why are you giving me this?" Nick asked, thinking that this situation was all too convenient.

"My father trusts you and I know we've had our differences, but you are still like family. I know you understand this situation, and how important it is to protect us."

Nick noticed that there was a degree of remorse in Ashraf's voice as he spoke and a part of him felt some sort of empathy. There was a glimmer of the friend he once knew speaking with grief about the family that did not treat him as well as he expected, but the one that he had belonged to, defended and loved. Nick fought the compulsion to place an arm on Ashraf. He tucked the envelope under his arm and said, "Thanks," to Ashraf as he did.

"Nick," Ashraf called out as Nick turned to exit the office. "For Adilaah."

Nick considered the words for a moment and smiled vaguely at Ashraf.

~

He could sense what McNeill would say before he dialled the phone, but Nick felt he had better keep the Superintendent in the loop on such an important development. He sat in bumper-to-bumper traffic as he held the phone to his ear, almost choking from the fumes emanating through the open window and sweating in the midday heat. The ringtone only repeated twice before he heard the stoic voice of his boss on the other end of the line.

"Superintendent it's D-C Shankar," Nick said quickly as he cleared his throat.

"What can I do for you Detective?" McNeill groaned.

"Sir, I have a lead on a suspect in the Khan murder," Nick announced proudly, shouting above the sound of the noisy traffic that surrounded his car.

"And?" McNeill replied abruptly.

"A Kurdish illegal named Nadir Suleiman sleeping rough in Kings Cross area," Nick continued.

"Is it reliable?" McNeill questioned.

"Well that's just it sir. The information came from Mr Khan's son, Ashraf, claiming that a witness came to them with the suspects whereabouts," Nick affirmed.

"So, what's the problem? Proceed with the arrest," McNeill said bluntly.

"With all due respect sir, I find it very convenient that the victim's family managed to produce a witness, suspect and whereabouts, all before we did," Nick declared confidently.

"You mean before you did," McNeill scoffed, "The Khans have a vested interest in finding their daughter's murderer and committing their influence to doing so."

"Yes, sir but…" Nick intermated nervously.

"We welcome their input detective," McNeill said deliberately.

Nick remained silently as he realised that his protest was largely inconsequential.

"I hope that I haven't misjudged you," McNeill said with a tone of disappointment.

"Not at all sir…" Nick shuffled.

But his words were wasted. McNeill had already hung up and he realised that to keep the newly found status he would have to silence his nagging voice and continue with this lead as though it had made its way strictly through police procedure, rank and file. He sunk deeper into the seat of his car as the traffic reflected his demeanour. He was stagnant and going nowhere.

11

Nick did not know this part of the city well. He had visited Kings Cross on many an occasion, but as for local street knowledge he was clueless. Although McNeill had wasted no time in signing the arrest warrant for his suspect Nadir Sulieman, it took several more hours to mobilise a tactical squad. Nick always loathed dealing with tactical and preferred to do things by himself. Besides the tactical team always seemed to 'drag' their heals when it came to dealing with CID, and Nick had to didactically fill in reams of paperwork that probably was a waste of time. However, he had no choice but to subscribe to the procedural bureaucracy if he was to get things moving.

The sun had become obscured by a dark grey blanket of cloud which seemed to make the city dense and stifling. Nick squatted in the recess of a doorway, on a litter strewn side street, which seemed to stink of vile sewer water. The stench was pungent enough to make Nick heave and empty the contents of his meagre lunch all over the small pavement. He reached into his back pocket of his denim jeans and removed a packet of gum. Quickly he unwrapped the confection and goggled up the minty relief, which managed to abate the churn in his stomach. Nick returned his gaze toward a set of arches that stood below a wide railway bridge that led to King's Cross station. Every few minutes the deafening squeal of train wheels on protesting track shook the structure. Within the arches lay piles of strapped cardboard boxes ready for recycling, mixed with red bags of shredded paper. Nick could see the outline of several figures in the daylight starved alcoves. He stretched his neck out further to see if he could spot his suspect. But Nadir was nowhere to be seen.

Nick turned his head to gaze in the direction of the two undercover officers who accompanied him. Both stood at the top of the street as it branched off from a busy main road. One of the men shook their head at him, signalling that they had not spotted him either.

Nick sat back into his sprawl on the street in exasperation.

Was the intel that Ashraf fed him reliable? Or was he just wasting his time? A cruel backlash for the things that had happened in the past.

These were just some of the thoughts that raced through his frenzied mind. He took a deep breath as he stood up and looked back the officers. Then he ignored the tactical plan and made a determined march for the arches.

Nick looked back at his back up officers as he reseeded into the dull recesses. The musty odour of rubbish and mucky, unwashed bodies greeted him. Nick could count fourteen men of various ethnic backgrounds lying on the ground or seated in makeshift chairs. Society's garbage had become their only possessions. Expressions of fear and rejection filled their dejected faces as Nick ventured further into the underworld that was hidden from view. This was London's shameless offspring, lurking in seedy corners throughout the city. They were the rejects of a social machine that was primed to produce only one type of fruitful citizen. These men who defied the mould were cast out and forced to live a subterranean existence, like parasites on overfed cattle, fighting for the scraps that fell from the devouring jaws of excess. Nick could only pity them and it made him realise how minor his problems really were. Each face told a different story, some pathetic, some scornful and some pious.

But none of these faces resembled his suspect and soon he had come to the end of the arches which had a small hole in the brickwork that led to an overgrown clearing. Nick thought to himself that he had nothing to lose if he looked through it, so with a minor flutter in his gut, he crouched down and slowly stuck his head through the crawl space, arching his back through.

The daylight shone down as his head emerged

on the other side, and he panned his head around. A few metres away he caught sight of a figure. Nick focused his eyes on the man, who was dressed in tatty trousers, secondhand shirt, blue blazer and plastic sandals. Nick immediately recognised the face as his eyes made contact with those of the man.

It was his suspect Nadir!

They both recognised each other. Nick scampered through the hole as quickly as he could, just as Nadir sprung to his feet and darted his eyes around searching for an escape.

Nick emerged from the hole, almost on all fours, just as Nadir stopped along a brick ledge with a six-metre drop. Nadir turned to look at his pursuer's progress then took a deep breath and leapt off the ledge, landing and rolling effortlessly in the long fluffy grass below, like some invincible action hero. Nick stopped at the ledge and froze as the height became apparent. He watched as his suspect clawed his way up an embankment along waves of green bush. He could not risk losing him, Nick thought to himself, and summoned up all the courage he could muster and made his leap. His landing was less graceful, and he landed with a pronounced thud that was felt by the sudden sharp pain in his right knee. Nick clasped on the thick of the bush and pulled himself to his feet, as he watched Nadir near the top of the bank. Nick ignored the intensifying ache in his knee and scissor sprung up the bank.

By now the two plain clothes officers had gaged the chase and ran up to meet Nadir on the opposite side of the busy arterial roadway. Nadir saw them and hopped over the steel barrier as cars whizzed by, racing down the road in the opposite direction of the approaching officers, dodging the oncoming cars.

Nick finally reached the top of the grassy embankment as he watched Nadir running between speeding vehicles and narrowly missing being run over. Nick gazed over at the two officers who were trying to stop traffic and cross over to intercept his fleeing suspect. Nick hopped over the barrier, realising that he had no option – lose the suspect or see him mounted by a speeding car, which meant a dead suspect. He dismissed the pain in his knee and pursued along the non-existent pavement beside the road.

Nadir had seen a brief break in the flow of traffic and cut across to the central reservation, as he stopped to look back at the persistent Nick and the other two officers, getting closer. In a blind panic Nadir stepped into the street and suddenly a car slammed into him launching him off his feet, rolling him over the bonnet, and crunching into the windshield. The car came to a screeching halt, as the bewildered driver stared at Nadir sprawled across it.

Nick arrived at the car as the rest of traffic began to slow and stop. Nadir was alive and breathing, but unconscious. Nick leant slowly on the side of the car as the other officers arrived on the scene. His heart was pounding, and he could barely get enough oxygen into his weary lungs but at least he had something to show for his efforts.

~

Nick studied Nadir through the one-way glass window, as he sat stoically at a small steel table in the compact interrogation room. His knee was throbbing. He had not had the time to ice or administer any medication, and the pain seemed to amplify his contempt of the suspect. Running only made him seem guilty, and if the lead that Ashraf had furnished was false, then why did Nadir seem so naturally antagonistic. A pronounced floodlight bathed the suspect and several CCTV cameras were focused on him, catching every vital detail. Nick could see the edginess in the subject. Something told him that this was no average murder suspect, and the intent in his wrath filled eyes indicated he wanted to be in that room, almost like he was ready for a confrontation. Nadir had a dark complexion with chiselled high cheek bones, a solid jaw line and striking brown eyes. His hair and beard had overgrown but he was still recognisably handsome with coffee skin and strong defined physique.

Nick's introspection of the situation was brought to end as McNeil opened the door and breezed in with a sublime charisma.

"Is this the subject?" McNeill quizzed.

"Yes sir. Full name is Nadir Suleiman, a-k-a Ismail Kader," Nick answered briskly. "Interpol believes he might also be Imran Zaheer, wanted for an assault in Amsterdam. Traveling on a forged Egyptian passport. Entered at Harwich, June 2014."

"Where's this one from?" McNeill inquired with a tone of abhorrence.

"Iraq. Kurdish Sir. Twenty-two years old. Details are sketchy, but A-T-B think he was an informer to Saddam's Republican Guard," Nick answered diligently.

"Status?" McNeill barked.

"Two rejected asylum applications," Nick replied flatly.

"Should be sending him home in no time," McNeill smirked. "Let's see what he knows, shall we?"

Nick nodded as he closed the dossier and opened the door to the interrogation room slowly. He wasn't prepared for McNeill's close supervision of the case and while he understood his superior's political motivations, he couldn't understand why he would want to be present for the questioning of the suspect. It's almost as if McNeill had wanted the outcome of the questioning to go one way, and that was for Nadir to be guilty. That would illustrate the slick efficiency of Scotland Yard in a case of such high standing. McNeill could use it as a shining light with the media, demonstrating his leadership and vision was yielding results and he could persevere with his autocratic style of leadership. Of course, this would bode well for Nick – a young new ethnic-minority detective who attacked the case with such a ruthless sense of accomplishment and zeal. The grandeur of that outcome gave him premature goose bumps, but there was still the gnawing feeling at the pit of his stomach, which for some reason he could not dispel.

Nick entered the room and pulled out one of the chairs adjacent to Nadir and sat down. He placed the dossier in front of him and then lifted his head up making full eye contact with Nadir, almost as if they were opposing poker players trying to conceal their cards from each other. A few moments of silence passed as each glared at each other almost as if they were sworn enemies.

Nick then broke the engagement as he flipped open the dossier and gently removed a picture and placed it before Nadir. It was a picture of Adilaah's corpse.

"Explain your relationship with this woman," He said bluntly.

Nadir lowered his defiant stance as he studied the picture and the grief on his face betrayed his indignation as he placed his hand on the glossy image almost as if he was touching the real body.

"You do know her," Nick persisted. "That's because you killed her!"

"I want a solicitor," Nadir said calmly.

"Only the guilty need solicitors," Nick replied.

Nick placed a digital recorder on the table and activated it. A voice spoke; "There's a dead girl. She's in Flat 42, 322 Great Cambridge Road. Come quickly."

"That's your voice. You made the call a few minutes after the time of death. After you fled the scene?" Nick said furtively as he cast his eyes onto the picture of Adilaah's lifeless corpse. Then he gazed back at Nadir who had looked back at Nick with a feeling of remorse. Then without provocation, a bottled fury seemed to erupt from the pit of Nick's being. In his mind, Nick saw Adilaah's smashed skull mixed in with the image of her lingering beauty as she stared back at him from his memory. He saw how Nadir in a spurt of malevolence picked up the Islamic Sculpture and pound into his beloved's head. He launched out of his seat and grabbed Nadir by the scruff of his muscular neck and slammed his surprised face onto the table. He felt like doing it again and again, until the murdering Cretan would plead out a confession, and Nick might then decide to stop. But then he realised that the session was being recorded on CCTV while McNeill watched, and he abated, bringing the suspect up face-to-face with his own.

"You killed her, didn't you?" Nick growled.

"I didn't kill her," Nadir spoke patiently, "But I can tell you who did Nick."

Nick let go of Nadir as he realised that he had

known much more than he led on and indeed the encounter had a personal agenda. He sat down slowly, composing himself as the air of police professionalism returned. He glanced over at the black glass showing only his own pallid reflection.

"I know everything. About you. About Adilaah. Your whole affair," Nadir whispered, realising he had the gobsmacked detective exactly where he wanted him.

12

Nick was unsure if McNeill had caught Nadir's end remarks, but he could not see him as he swiftly instructed that Nadir be taken back down to the cells. He was panicked that Nadir's knowledge of his and Adilaah's affair would jeopardise the whole case and leave him smeared in the process. Nadir could only be held for twenty-four hours before he had to be charged or released, and it was only a matter of time before they had to let him have access to counsel, and no doubt he would use his knowledge to plea bargain.

This would expose the case to all sorts of scrutiny, including his qualification and experience in dealing with a case of this magnitude, not to mention the knowledge of the affair finding its way back to Mahmoud and Ashraf, who he knew wouldn't act so sublimely as he might have liked. Also, there was a good chance that he might unwittingly find himself a suspect, sinking deeper into this tangled web of deceit, ending up fired and in the very same cell block as Nadir.

As he walked down the brightly lit corridor with rows of formidable iron doors to the holding cells, Nick couldn't help but feel like a puppet in a drama that seemed to be enacted without his control, and he knew Nadir's bombshell would have catastrophic consequences.

Nick painfully limped along the buffed vinyl floor, accompanied on his journey by a chirpy, portly prison officer who had a curiously cheery disposition. He had rambled on about his fondness for gardening as Nick tried to sift through his fleeting thoughts. Nick wondered what real use this old-timer would be if he was suddenly overcome by the inmates, and how his passion for gardening would help fend off a vicious onslaught. Nevertheless, the old man's advice for maintaining a perfectly pruned and pert rose garden in the face of uncertain climate held a particular resonance for him. Nick envied the humble gardener as he studied the man's nametag reading a contrite – Stanley.

"The trick is," Stanley laboured on. "Give your roses plenty of love." He looked directly into Nick's searching eyes. Nick couldn't help but feel that Stanley's droll words were lined with a hidden meaning. Maybe he was trying to tell him the rose was a symbol for the truth, and in the midst of adversity, it could only thrive with unconditional love. Or perhaps, the rose was Adilaah and his love for her was the testament to adversity and in that he would find truth. On the other hand, perhaps, those words were simply the ramblings of an overzealous, slightly senile old fool who shouldn't be taken too seriously. Nick was too tired to figure it out at this point.

The sun was setting through the sparse sets of windows as the duo stopped in front of the cell door that housed Nadir. Stanley peered in the tiny window on the door to ensure all was safe to enter, and then with shaking hands inserted a key and unclicked the cumbersome door.

Nick walked slowly into the glib and tiny cell to find Nadir kneeling on a prayer matt facing what little he could see of the diminishing sun in devout prayer. Stanley retreated behind him leaving the two men alone in the cell as Nick courteously waved him off. It was against policy to be alone in a cell with a suspect, but Nick's humane pleas, and the promise of a bottle of Single Malt to the Captain of the guards managed to allow him a few minutes of privacy. He hoped that alone in his cell, Nadir might be more cooperative and eager to tell him the truth behind Adilaah's murder, which might help him silence the nagging doubt he had over Nadir's involvement.

Nick strolled in cautiously as he surveyed the meagre contents of the cell. Nadir had been permitted a shower and was issued the prison-standard grey sweatshirt and trousers, which was decidedly more comfortable and cleaner than his indigent street wear. He was now clean shaven and had sculpted his black hair into a flowing mane along the back of his head. Nick waited patiently as Nadir continued to bow in ritual toward the sun concluding his prayer.

"I'm glad you came," He said as he opened his eyes. "Sit." Nadir offered.

Hesitantly Nick moved to a chair that stood across from the bed and, with relief, slid into it taking the weight of his aching leg. Nadir got to his feet, rolled up his prayer mat and placed it neatly on the bed, as he sat down. He was much taller than Nick and sat with a purposeful poise that told Nick he had probably served in the military and was of some standing.

"I didn't kill her," Nadir confirmed calmly.

"Witness testimony says otherwise," Nick replied.

"I loved her," Nadir admitted as Nick stared at him. "So did you."

Nick stared at Nadir unsure of how to reply.

"Don't be so surprised. Everyone loved her," Nadir exclaimed. "Anyway, she told me."

"How did you meet?" Nick probed, attempting to maintain his composure.

"Street shelter. She helped me get off the street. She arranged that flat through her connections. We started to talk, then meet and you know…" Nadir reflected dourly. "She loved to read poetry."

"Adilaah wouldn't…" Nick intervened, dismissing Nadir's story.

"Associate with me? Why?" Nadir protested.

"Because I have nothing! That is what she needed, someone to treat her like a person. I had nothing to give her and nothing to take from her. Just respect for who she truly was."

Nadir went silent as his emotions cracked his stoic exterior and his eyes became glassy as he stared out the small window. The light haloed his prominent features and Nick could tell that there was a weight of truth in his words, almost as if the recollection of Adilaah's form brought salvation that bathed his weary soul.

Nick somehow felt the same emotion building, weakening his disparaging resolve as he spoke.

"So what happened?"

"You know what happened!" Nadir snapped as he gazed purposefully at Nick.

"The brother?" Nick questioned with slight dread.

Nadir nodded slowly as the ugly truth settled in.

"For what reason?" Nick argued.

"Self-preservation. Honour. Think about it. Adilaah's body was conveniently found in the flat where we are seen together. And how did you find me?" Nadir countered.

"Ashraf. Said a witness came forward," Nick blurted.

"A witness who is being influenced. How hard with that be for them?" Nadir reasoned.

"It doesn't make sense. Besides its your word

against theirs. And there's enough in the docket to charge you!" Nick pointed out.

"Then they have won, and Adilaah, the truth, my innocence will be lost," Nadir exclaimed despondently.

"I can't do anything. I'm sorry," Nick responded blankly.

"You can. Adilaah was once beaten within an inch of her life. She had to go to hospital and a police statement was taken. Check your files."

"There's nothing in her files. Believe me I've checked," Nick retorted.

"It's there. Just hidden away. Only one man could have enough influence with the police to have them buried to protect his public reputation." Nadir declared.

"Mahmoud…" Nick muttered slowly trusting his nagging intuition.

Nadir nodded, realising the implications of his accusation. Nick rose from his chair and slowly walked over to the cell door, and then stopped before asking bleakly.

"Is it yours?"

"What?" Nadir replied cluelessly.

"The baby," Nick said firmly as he faced Nadir again.

"She was pregnant?" Nadir smirked dismissively, as he stared at the stark floor, considering the revelation. "I doubt it. We never went that far…"

"You almost had me convinced," Nick scoffed and waved at the CCTV in the cell.

"I didn't want to do it this way, but she was wearing it," Nadir waxed furtively as the amicable tone became antagonistic once more.

"What?" Nick answered defensively.

"The locket. The one you gave her. She was wearing it when she was murdered. It's evidence now, isn't it?" Nadir continued.

Nick stared at Nadir with animosity, realising that he was being extorted, as he clearly recalled the Gold Locket around Adilaah's body at the scene of the murder.

"I'll have no choice but to tell them you gave it to her. Your whole affair will become public. Mahmoud will know. You will become a suspect. Your career will be over before it even began," Nadir said calmly as he lay down on the bed.

"I'll leave you to think about it." He said before he shut his eyes and went to sleep, quite proud of himself.

Nick could feel frustration building within him. He was in a corner and had nowhere to turn. Nadir knew he had Nick exactly where he wanted him, and he would happily sacrifice the detective and his entire warped existence in favour of saving his skin. Frustration evolved into a bloodthirsty rage and Nick kicked the scuffed white wall with fury as the pious Stanley locked the cell door behind him, leaving the poor old man with a pronounced fright. Nick marched off as he desperately sought solitude and a means to organise his thoughts along with his next move. And there weren't any that were that appealing.

~

The flat was pokey and compact, and Nick detested living in it, especially when he had Adilaah around. The peeling wallpaper and worn carpet always made him feel somewhat inadequate compared to her opulent lifestyle, and although she constantly told him that she didn't care where they were, as long as they were together, it still bothered him. He imagined that someday, when he completed his training at the academy, he would move out of this poverty and into a luxurious new flat and show her the life that she was accustomed to. Nick had always wanted to be a detective, just like on TV, and he watched every show he could, trying to emulate his heroes. He was never lonely for he had Jessica Fletcher, Inspector Morse or Columbo to keep him company and provide him with the irreverent raw material and motivation that he needed in his ambition. An ambition that satisfied the emptiness that was left by his constantly working father or the legacy of an absent mother. In the mind of a young boy, he didn't need them, for as long as he had his TV heroes, whose world he could escape into, his drab misery endowed life did not seem so bad.

But tonight, she was with him, and he wasn't going to waste any time on his melancholic thoughts, but rather engross himself in her for as long as he could before she had to run off and be whisked back into her make-believe prison.

Nick took Adilaah's hand and held it as they sat at a small wobbly kitchen table. He gently caressed the palm of her hand as he placed a small velvet black box into it.

"What's this?" Adilaah asked with wonder. She stared at the box in her hand for a moment as she contemplated the contents.

"Open it," Nick encouraged.

She looked at him longingly and parted her luscious lips, sweetly smiling, overwhelmingly touched by the gesture. She ran her finger along the bevelled edge and lifted the lid. Inside lay a shimmering antique Gold Heart-Shaped Locket with a tiny off set red ruby.

"It's lovely," Adilaah exclaimed, as if it were the most beautiful thing in the world.

"My father gave it to my mother," Nick confirmed. "Of course she gave it back when he left."

Adilaah studied it, awestruck by its authentic beauty.

"Here," Nick said, as he removed the necklace and placed it around her slender neck, stroking her hair and shoulders as he sat back to admire the perfect combination of her auburn beauty and the jewel.

"You'll always have my heart," He said blissfully, his chest heavy with love.

13

The Imam's monosyllabic words echoed as he recited the Janazah prayer. Nick stood a few rows from the front but could still see the funeral ritual. His knee throbbed with pain as he tried to take the weight of it, hobbling in the trimmed wet grass. The sun was reluctantly trapped behind a veil of clouds which made the air fresh and damp from the previous night's rain. He was surrounded by almost a hundred men-only members of the extended Khan family which meant a desperate competition for personal space. Beside him stood his resolute boss McNeill, motionless and frozen. Nick closed his coat snuggly dispelling the brisk morning air as he scanned the attendees. Many of London's most wealthy and influential people had put in an appearance, which intimidated Nick somewhat. His scan stopped on the two figures, prominently stood next to the Imam. Nick focused his attention on them examining their reactions for some trace of remorse, but there was none. He wondered whether they felt triumphant that their complex plan to commit the murder of their daughter had helped them keep their position and standing.

To the many high-rollers that stood next to him, they must have seemed like two pious, righteous and upright pillars who were simply mourning the loss of what was the antithesis to their ideal and illusion. Truth and purity that was the only thing at the heart of Adilaah's being, and she became expendable in a bid to uphold their lie. Worst of all, Nick was now a part of that lie. He had sipped from the same poisonous cup and in that elixir was the corruption and conspiracy that he had willed for through his own blind ambition. And that made him feel sick with disgust, for he stood at a crossroads; maintain this treachery and allow an innocent man to be convicted as the true assailants go free. All the while becoming notorious for his self-serving rise to stardom, by being in league with the very people whom he swore to put away. Or he could act and inflict justice. A part of him told him to let sleeping dogs lie and reap his ill-gotten gains with apathetic glory. But another part told him that he could not allow any of this to persist. And that part had gone from a whisper, to the voice of an operatic tenor.

The Imam had concluded his prayer and family members began to offer their condolences to Mahmoud and Ashraf. The coffin began its shadowy descent into the red carpet covered ground. Nick felt his emotion churn from the centre of his chest and lodge itself in his throat like an iron weight, but he did his best to restrain it. Adilaah's ghost still haunted his thoughts, so for him, her spirit lived while her body was laid to rest.

~

Nick took particular delight in watching her dress, despite knowing it was the end of another brief encounter and he would have to let her go again, back to her father and that world that he was an outsider to.

"You haven't told him yet, have you?" Nick asked with particular emphasis.

"What do you expect me to tell him?" Adilaah replied defensively. "By the way Dad, you know that Driver who used to work for us, well I'm shagging his son…"

"He'd have something to worry about if it were actually shagging," Nick said sarcastically as she finished clipping her bra and placing the straps over her shoulder. He had never seen her impatient or angry before, so this was one of those rare occasions where her tempered passion was brought to bear. She looked at him with daggers in her eyes as her shapely figure stood before him and he looked at her full bosom, flat stomach and smooth toned thighs, as she searched around for her blouse.

"You don't get it do you? My father's whole life is his faith and honour. And there's no way that his daughter, his obedient, respectful and supposedly moral apple of his eye, is going to be seen to betray that," Adilaah declared loudly, as she buttoned her blouse. "He would rather see me in a grave. And let me tell you, if he found out about this, that's precisely where I would end up with no one to mourn me!"

Nick who had been reclining defiantly in bed, sat up with a purpose. "You forget one thing in all of this Adilaah, that you have a choice. You can choose how you want to live your life, choose your own fate. Even one with me!"

Adilaah scoffed at Nick's reply and sulked while she draped the Hijab over her head.

"You don't understand," Adilaah spoke afflicted. "This *is* my only choice." She finished adjusting her Hijab on her head and marched out the door, slamming it behind her.

~

Adilaah's voice echoed over his thoughts, as Nick looked at the faces of Ashraf and Mahmoud with unbridled contempt. Then he shifted his gaze over to McNeil's blank expression. Nick fought back his tears as he slowly pushed passed the hordes of mourners who had begun to leave. He stopped before the pit of the grave and gazed at the sight of Adilaah's solitary white coffin. Inside lay all his regrets, hopes and, the emotion that he had not experienced with anyone else, love.

It made his heart swell and his eyes fill with tears. The emotion was too much, and a tear streamed down his cheek. He slowly placed his hand into his black overcoat and produced a partially opened ruby-red rose bud. Just like their love it had not full bloomed, and remained stunted and subdued, but for him it retained all of its inherent beauty and magnificence. Nick held it over the coffin and let go. The flower dropped and landed dead centre, almost as if it had seared itself to the coffin for the rest of her eternal journey, like an immovable relic. Nick took a deep breath as he lifted his heavy head. Mahmoud and Ashraf stared at his ritual and then at him. There was something unpredictable about the look in his eyes, almost as if it was something they had not expected. There was resolution in his eyes, forged in the foundry of dormant righteousness. He stared at them with petulant vengeance and they seemed to harbour an unusual feeling of fear. Nick smiled knowingly at them. They returned his gesture with scorn.

~

Nick felt no conviction in returning to the office and the reality that came with it. He was avoiding dealing with Nadir and the charges that McNeill would no doubt expect in order to neatly close the case. He needed some respite, and as he sat in the painted green hallway of the Nursing Home, he thought that he chose an odd place to find it.

The woe of the funeral still lay heavily upon him and he found it difficult to dispel the melancholy. He stared at the profusely mundane light of the fluorescent lights lining the hallway, and it seemed to catalyse his grief for Adilaah. In his head there was no strategy that would end well. In fact, he felt like he possessed the ignition and fuel that would tear down many lives, including his own. It was as if Adilaah came back into his life to set him on a radical course correction, a catharsis that, through her death, would purge through all of the discord with a fire of purity, pain and grief.

"Hello, are you Mr Shankar's son?" the plump middle-aged Afro-Caribbean Nurse inquired.

"Yes. How is he?" Nick replied as he quickly sprung to his feet.

"He's better today. His blood pressure was really high, but it's stabilized. He'll be pleased to see you." The Nurse replied with a warm smile.

Rohit lay restfully in his sturdy metal framed bed, looking frail and diminutive, almost as if there wasn't much of his body languishing under the covers. The room smelled stuffy and suffocating, shrouded in a sense of death much like the ceremony that Nick had just come from. He approached his sleeping father slowly, watching him breathing with great difficulty in a shallow heave. He studied his father's form. Rohit had shrunk into half the man he was. He could always remember how his father towered over him with his strong build. His father had always told him stories of his life in the Indian army before he returned to civilian life, and Nick could tell his father deeply missed the discipline and order. Rohit had joined the army because his life was missing just that – order. He had come from a long line of 'Walas' – street traders who did everything from selling tea on the street to doing laundry just to get by. Rohit spent the best part of his life on the street, getting in all sorts of trouble until the time when he was fifteen or sixteen, he was implicated in the robbery of a wealthy English madam. But rather than sentence the boy to one of Delhi's already overcrowded jails, a sympathetic magistrate ordered that the boy be conscripted into the British Indian Army as a stretcher boy and sent to North Africa to fight the Germans and Italians. Carrying so many wounded men to and from the medical camps, and dealing with the tragedy of war, made Rohit strong and powerful. But that was not the man who lay in the bed before Nick.

"Dad," Nick said softly as he placed a comforting hand on his shoulder.

"Who is it?" Rohit answered feebly.

"It's Narendra," Nick replied.

"You didn't need to come all the way here just to see me," Rohit implied.

"I wanted to," Nick said as Rohit simmered into a quiet calmness.

"Is mum coming?" Rohit asked in a confused tone.

"No," Nick answered becoming impatient at Rohit's estranged mind.

"Oh," Rohit answered disappointed. "I wish she would come."

Nick looked at Rohit sadly as he watched his father drift off to sleep again, feeling like he had lost his father, and what remained was the remnants of the man that faded in and out of consciousness. The only living presence of the sum of his entire life was the barely alert shell that lay before him. He tried to afford more generosity, for the man had single-handedly raised him from an infant and given him everything that he could afford. He desperately wanted to resurrect the relationship that he once knew, the one that was just him and his father, when they were a unit trying to survive the hostile world that seemed to want to pull them apart. The sight of this solitary old man made Nick feel alone like he had never felt before. He needed his father – the man who seemed to have a fractured solution or piece of wisdom for him no matter what the dilemma, despite his resistance to it.

"I made Detective," Nick announced at his dozing father. "I thought you might want to know." Nick paused in silence. "Thought you might be proud of me," he continued.

Nick took a deep cleansing breath and sat slowly on the bed, relieving his painful knee.

"Truth is, I'm in a real bind. I've done some

things. I've lied. Covered up a murder. Now I'm about to convict an innocent man and let the perpetrators walk free," Nick slowly spoke. "You shouldn't be proud of me. I'm not proud of me," Nick admitted.

Nick felt the delicate touch of Rohit's hand on his arm.

"You know your Teachers used to call me to school and say, that boy is such a troubled boy. So shy and so quiet. He doesn't play with the other children. And I used to say to them. Naren is a gentle boy, but when he is ready, he will be the man he wants to be," Rohit muttered and then smiled at Nick, before falling off to sleep again.

His father's words reassured him. He leant down and kissed his father on the forehead, something he had never done before. But he wanted the old man to know that he was grateful, not just for those words, but for everything he had done for him.

14

"Nadir is dead," McNeill announced plainly without any attached remorse.

"What?" Nick exclaimed with shock cutting through his estranged voice. "How did this happen?"

"Used the strands from his prayer mat," McNeill replied indignantly.

Nick's heart sank as he stared out of McNeill's large office window into the dark greyness that seemed to seize the daylight. He felt an overwhelming sense of despair eclipse him and while he thought this made things simpler for him, he couldn't help but feel that this outcome wasn't the right one. It was certainly convenient for him, as Nadir's knowledge of Nick and Adilaah's affair would go with him to the grave, but he couldn't shake the sense of obligation that strangely seemed to persist in his agitated gut. He felt like expounding his emotion into a deliberate voice that would release his frustration, but instead he remained silent, and his very calm introspective seemed only to incense the

Superintendent, making him un-characteristically unnerved and edgy.

"Left this," McNeill rambled, sloppily tossing a transparent plastic jacket that contained Nadir's note over to Nick.

"He had probable cause. He had motive and was photographed with the victim," McNeill continued with a tone that seemed like that of a rambling salesman.

"Motive?" Nick enquired furtively, as McNeill ignored the detective's abrupt interruption and continued.

"His DNA matches the scene. And of course, the 9-9-9 call," McNeill declared as he noted Nick's insubordinate manner and paced coolly from behind the refuge of his ominous desk to confront Nick.

"You did a good job," McNeill remarked as his frosty outlook warmed.

Nick looked the Superintendent in the eye and said cynically. "Did I?"

"Yes. Not bad for your first week," McNeill expressed. "I'm authorising a few days off. You deserve it."

Nick felt the remark as somewhat condescending as he watched McNeill return to his desk, revelling in the triumph of his political weaving. He had got exactly what he wanted. An ally in Mahmoud Khan and a detective to do his bidding no matter what that entailed. The thought made Nick feel used and dirty, fouled with a stench that he could not remove. He could not even bring himself to wonder how it is that Nadir could go from the righteous stalwart to a remorseful weakling that could take his own life. He knew that McNeill was capable of treachery to further his own warped ambitions, but murderer? That was a step too far.

Nadir however, was the perfect choice for a suspect. Alone and indigent, a refugee with no fixed abode that the city streets would be happy to be rid of. He knew how McNeill would spin it too. Nadir's threat of blackmail was not just putting Nick's reputation on the line, it was putting the whole of Scotland Yard in jeopardy, including his own. And there was no way he was going to let someone of Nadir's lowly stature smear him, let alone be responsible for another enquiry, which would certainly leave Nick on the wrong side of the firing line. He sensed that McNeill, in a strange twist of loyalty, had protected him, while protecting the whole police force. That day in the interrogation room, he had heard enough of Nadir's words to put something into play, a strategy that involved the absolution of this. He knew if poked around and asked his gardening enthusiast Stanley, who had been in to see Nadir, that it would point straight to his partner Ron. He was the only one that McNeill had enough leverage on, that would make Ron take care of things rather 'bluntly' as he put it.

Nick looked closely at Nadir's blood scrolled letter and read the words:

'thou hast said that thou wilt torment me, but I shall fear not such a warning.

For where thou art, there can be no torment, and where thou art not, how can such a place exist?'

Nick turned around and opened the door, leaving McNeill without even being dismissed. The words resonated through his very soul. He had read them before.

~

Nick could not to even understand what prompted him to do it, but suddenly he found himself before Miles Monroe's aluminium office door. He wrapped softly on the bleak frosted glass as he heard a muffled, "Come in," from within.

Nick gripped the handle with purpose and placed his weight behind it as he pushed the unusually stiff door.

"You said your door is always open," Nick remarked grimly as he approached Miles who was seated, crouching low in front of his desk, as though the workload was weighted squarely on his flaccid shoulders. Miles peered up at Nick, unsure of what to make of this visit.

"Sit," Miles gestured with a mild manner.

"I'm fine," Nick answered resiliently. "The Khan murder. The suspect hanged himself."

"I know," Miles replied coolly.

"I just think that…" Nick stammered. "I mean I…"

Nick took a deep breath as he summoned enough courage to complete a coherent sentence.

"It's quite unnerving isn't it? When you can't tell your friends from your enemies," Miles remarked as he reclined back into his chair, placing his hands behind his head as they touched the window ledge strewn with scruffy potted plants.

"There are always plenty of people who want to make allegiances with you on the way up," Miles continued. "But not on the way down."

Nick grimaced as he watched Miles smirk and open a desk drawer, before removing an article he had curled up in his pale fist. Miles looked at Nick sardonically, dangling the Gold Locket Chain that he had once placed around Adilaah's neck. Nick looked at the chain with disbelief. Somehow the Prosecutor held it in his hands. The very thing that Nadir had threatened him with flayed about mockingly in front of him.

"Exquisite," Miles exclaimed as he gazed at the jewel. "An antique no less. With a remarkable history. Belonged to the British Ambassador to India in fifty-eight. Reported stolen, only to end up around his daughter's neck, whom as it turns out is your mother."

Miles held up a plain brown dossier. Nick stared at it with trepidation. Then he gingerly took hold of it and opened the document, scanning the contents. He didn't need to read the detail. His eyes simply went to the header. It read; *Testimony of Carley Anne Banks*.

She had signed it. His heart sank.

"Hell, hath no fury as a woman scorned," Miles lamented as Nick stood, mortified by the Prosecutor's words. "She didn't receive a Gold Locket necklace after all she's fucking done for you! Her words, not mine."

Miles looked at Nick somewhat sympathetically.

"She felt she needed to tell me everything," Miles spoke blithely. "For your own good."

Nick believed that when Carley left that morning, she would simply come back after a few days. She always did. But perhaps she sensed it, in the way he had described his determination to bring Adilaah's murderer to justice. She was more than just a murder victim to him, and that it was personal. Despite her hard and sometimes brutal exterior, deep down she was remarkably perceptive, and all it took for her to turn on him was for Miles to show her what she was denied – a token of his love – the necklace. And Miles knew it was enough to undo Nick's entire account of Tyson.

Nick stood horrified and lost for words, trying to conceal his disappointment at Carley's betrayal.

Miles returned the gold necklace back to its resting place in the desk drawer.

"I couldn't care less about your entanglements with the Khan girl. Her father might, but I have no cause to upset him, especially when things have been so amicably concluded," Miles laboured. "But, what I do care about is what really happened that night with Tyson and Allen. And you have to decide what side you want to be on."

"I never thought that you would be capable of such…" Nick said with a reprehensive tone.

"Deceit? I play the best hand from the cards I'm dealt. And not by choice mind you," Miles quickly interjected with an air of scorn.

Nick took a moment to consider his situation then exited the office. There was nothing more to be said. He felt as though he was in the eye of an unforgiving storm with no hope of pardon.

In the distance, Ron watched with malevolent suspicion.

~

Mahmoud sat on a bench in a secluded brush growth with a veiled composure. He surveyed the large boating lake before him with a casual admiration. He had always relished these expansive green spaces in the city, something that he did not experience as a child growing up in arid rural Pakistan. He had always dreamt of it. The majestic sway of trees in the coaxing wind, delicate wild flowers carpeting the forest floor and cool glassy water ebbing in the glorious brooding lake. Regents park presented a splendour that elevated his weary mind, transporting him away from his responsibility and obligation.

Here he felt like an ordinary person, not the forthright leader that had expectation and honour thrust upon him. Here he was at peace. But that was not to last.

He watched as McNeill approached, walking with the stance that only someone who was trying to hide deeper inferiority would do. An upright, stiff and unreasoning reproach filled with a wary stolid expression. Mahmoud sensed that McNeill only tolerated their association because there was something to be gained from it, and he knew that once that was through, McNeill would turn from ally to foe, regarding him and his kind as an unwelcome intrusive plague to be viewed with suspicion and distrust.

"Odd that we should meet like this," McNeill re-marked as he sat down slowly beside Mahmoud.

"It's a beautiful day Mr McNeil. I thought we could enjoy it," Mahmoud replied as he admired the clear blue sky.

"Quite," McNeill said with a stiff upper lip, eager to get his business with Mahmoud under way.

"What of our arrangement," Mahmoud inquired.

"As planned," McNeill replied curtly.

"Indulge my curiosity. And my family matter, what about the Iraqi?"

"Won't be of any further harm to anyone. Especially your family or your name," McNeill declared diligently. "Now indulge my curiosity."

"The Iraqi was recruited by them last year. My sources tell me that they were planning something large," Mahmoud waxed.

"Large?" McNeill asked solemnly.

"Something very close to home…" Mahmoud exclaimed slowly. "Very close."

"Scotland Yard?" McNeill protested. "Impossible."

"Think about it, a sleeper cell right inside Scotland Yard," Mahmoud pointed out as he handed McNeil a small brown envelope. "It's all in there."

"This concludes our arrangement," McNeill declared as he rose to his feet.

"Remember the boy is not to be tarnished by any of this," Mahmoud confirmed.

"Why do you choose to protect him?" McNeill inquired.

"A promise I made to his father," Mahmoud replied. "Besides he's like a son."

15

The breakfast rush was coming to an end as the café emptied of its usual patrons of truck drivers and construction labourers. The sun bathed the vacated tables in a hazy orange glow, highlighting the empty coffee cups, grease stained plates and crusty ketchup coated cutlery. Nick languished sombrely, tucked faraway in the back, close to the entrance of the only toilet in the building. The pungent smell of bleach mixed with the heady fumes of grilled bacon and fried eggs, about the only staple being served from the scant menu. He had been brooding at the table for over an hour occasionally sipping an over-brewed coffee that barely provided any respite from his drowsy sleep deprived state. His mind raced, and he tried to focus all of his fleeting thoughts to a particular one. He went over it again and again. And yet he still had trouble believing it. He knew that deep down he should have treated her better than he had, but he always felt that he rescued her from the life that she herself couldn't bring herself to escape. He had always strived to have a better life, elevating himself out of the life that his father did his best to provide for him. But he knew that he could do better. And maybe that is why he took the path that he did, as a means to get to where he was going. But she seemed to accept her place in the world. For her this was as good as it would get, for no matter how much she tried she could not shake it. And even the one time that she tried, it still evaded her.

Nick lifted his head from his lost gaze at the cream laminate table and over to the grimy wall-mounted clock. It was nine fourteen. Carley was late. He had not heard from her since that morning when she left without much to say to him. He was glad to be rid of her. That way he could focus his attention on the case. But now so much had changed in just a few days and he now felt different about everything. Even her.

Nick kept telling himself that maybe she had no choice and Miles had put her in a corner, and that's why she did it. But he knew that wasn't it. He knew her better than that. She was a survivor, and this was her way of making him recognise her true position in his life. She went to Miles because she wanted to make a point. Although he could not understand what that was yet. That is why he needed to find out and he wanted to hear the words from her mouth.

Carley burst in the door with brute force and swept through the dining room straight past the kitchen, avoiding the disapproving stare from the much too tolerant owner Rich. He was a small diminutive creature with a boney frame, greasy skin and hair, that looked as if it was soaked in the same lard that was used to cook his notorious heart stopping fry-ups. Still they had a reputation for being one of the best and Nick often devoured them after long ill-fated drinking binges, back when he drank with ferocity.

"Late night?" Rich inquired sarcastically, as Carley emerged flustered.

"Leave it out!" Carley announced loudly at Rich as she tied the straps of her pink frilly apron that sat in complete contrast to her plain purple top, baggy blue trousers and flat black shoes. She was uncharacteristically normally dressed, Nick thought, as she began clearing the messy tables and hadn't noticed him yet. Carley rushed back into the kitchen, her arms loaded with plates and cups. She was not naturally suited to this sort of work or any work for that matter and was never going to be the type to follow a career path that involved university, or any vocation that involved working behind a desk or in a team. She held a firm opinion on practically everything and very often it was not a popular one, nor did she take kindly to anyone who opposed or challenged her. She saw this as an outright challenge on her very being which resulted in a ferocious defence that would never warrant yielding. Lurking deep down though, she was someone who wanted her voice to be heard and to be taken seriously.

Carley emerged from the kitchen door with

prowess and was ready to attack the next set of tables when she saw Nick and froze. For a moment they watched each other, waiting for someone to break the ice. Nick did his best to maintain a decorum, but invariably the question of her betrayal needed to be answered.

"Why'd you do it?" Nick blurted in an insolent tone.

"Do what?" Carley replied sullenly.

"Munroe," Nick implied. "You went to see him."

Carley stared at Nick for a moment, unable to form the words to express her bleak, pallid feelings.

"You know why," she then said, as she moved to clear the table next to him. "Besides it's something you should have done in the first place."

"It's not that simple," Nick lamented.

"For me it is!" She replied irately.

"You have that luxury. I don't," Nick replied as he got to his feet.

"The truth is not a luxury!" Carley bellowed.

Their voices had filled the empty diner as Rich quietly retreated from the increasingly fiery exchange.

"It's our only way out," Carley declared despondently as she sat deflated at one of the tables. "From all of it!"

"What do you mean?" Nick inquired as he sat before Carley.

Carley hunched over the dirty table burying her agonized face in her hands.

"He needed a way to get to Tyson," Carley admitted. "And you were it."

"So I could take the blame?" Nick declared as he began to put things together.

"Your partner Ron's been a junkie for years, even dealing on the side for Tyson. Last year Tyson got linked on some dumb fucking burglary charge and he was going to talk. Give up Ron, Police corruption, the whole lot, including me," Carley said, as she wiped away her tears and looked Nick in the eye. "Serious prison time. They knew you would do what they wanted – lie to cover their tracks."

"They?" Nick questioned with hostility.

"McNeill," Carley replied.

"So, you used me like everyone else," Nick stated biliously, as Carley gazed back at him dolefully.

"Now you know what it feels like," Carley said woefully.

"I suppose we're even," Nick declared flatly. He rose to his feet and marched to the door.

Carley shut her eyes in despair as regret overtook her and the finality of Nick's words resonated through her being.

"I can make this right," Carley announced woefully. "Just tell me what you need."

Nick stopped in his tracks.

~

Carley looked upon the car park with apprehension. Ron's car was the only one in the middle of an array of marked bays amidst the surrounding woods. The woods were eerily silent apart from the icy wind that howled through them. She hadn't seen Ron in months and she was unsure of what to expect. She had always got along with Ron and he viewed her with some affection, but she knew that he saw her as an object and a means to get his way. Often that meant that she had to tolerate his sloppy advances and the occasional unwelcome grope. She dismissed it as a consequence of their relationship, but she would never let anything substantial develop out of it. However, there was a time when she would have let him have his way with her, just to be able to have a policeman in her corner, and that would have made her feel safe and secure. She hated herself for having to stoop so low just to feel a degree of security, but it seemed in her chequered life she had always needed to protect herself or have some sort of means to.

It all started when she was quite young, about eleven, and before she even took notice she began to parade the full figure of a girl aged sixteen. That immediately spurned that advances of boys much older than her, along with the jealousy of the girls too. Carley realised very quickly that she could use her new-found status to her advantage. She was never one to take her scholastic development seriously and very quickly she was failing in most of her subjects and was ordered to take an audience with the school principal. Carley knew that she would have to do something to prevent her fate being sealed into a life of menial labour, as she was kicked out of school and forced to join the ranks of the rest of her family working in the nearby steel mill. That was something she could not stand, and so she took the meeting wearing a short black skirt from the previous school year, and her sister's white shirt with gaping holes from where the buttons battled to stay together revealing her braless budding breasts. The aptly named Mr Peerless could barely contain his leering incoherent babbling as she sat cross-legged before him, exposing her smooth athletic thighs. From then on, she never had to worry about failing another class or being expelled from school again, as she took on the role of faculty-student liaison and spent most afternoons up against his filing cabinet while he mounted her from the rear. He was her first, and while her mother had told her to wait until she was in love, she didn't care, as it wasn't that important to her. Their affair carried on for many years and most of the school knew what was going on, but none dare break their silence. Mr Peerless would take Carley on long drives, buying her clothing and jewellery promising to leave his frigid wife for her, declaring his love for his Lolita. But then it all came to an abrupt end when Carley's Home Economics teacher refused to continue with the charade and blew the whistle.

As it turns out, he had had an affair with her too and promised her all the same things. Peerless was promptly sacked and Carley was expelled. Her parents then kicked her out and she was alone on the streets, in need of that security that she so desperately sought once more. It didn't come so easily at first as Carley encountered a string of engagements, even becoming the muse of a lesbian painter who would get off by painting surreal variations of her vagina disguised as ripe tropical fruit. But for Carley, that was enough, and it was the only form of love that she needed.

But then Carley met Tyson. In the beginning his machismo and bravado mesmerised her, and for a short time Carley thought that she loved him. But he had other ideas for her. She thought Crack was harmless at first, but she tried it anyway, and it seemed to take her to places that she had never been before. It seemed to bring all of her doubts and insecurities under control and she felt invincible, almost as if nothing would hurt her. But that initial taste became a regular occurrence and then it was an obsession that she could not do without. Once that happened, Tyson had her under his spell. He got her to do whatever he wanted, provided he gave her, her daily drug fix. Dealing. 'Muling'. And even being passed around Tyson's friends and customers to be used like a piece of meat. She was not proud of it. She knew now how far she had gone and the reprehensible things that she had done just to get high.

That was when she met Detective Ron Allen, and then soon after in a holy moment of clarity, she met Nick. The very sight of him made her detest herself and the life that she had assumed. The moment she lay her eyes on him she knew they were kindred spirits, and for the first time in her life she wanted to give, rather than take, protect rather than desecrate. She knew true love for the first time. She felt as though she was eleven again and the none of the unsavoury and degrading encounters had occurred. She finally knew what her bizarrely truthful alcoholic mother was talking about, for with Nick she felt like she was making love and not just 'fucking'.

That feeling of love overcame her once more as she thought about Nick, while pacing stoically to Ron's car, taking a deep breath as she opened the door.

Ron looked excited to see her and he gestured for her to get in. Carley nervously accepted, as she slid cautiously into the grey patterned bucket seats. The car smelled as though Ron had just had his dinner in it, as the aroma of chicken Kebab permeated.

"Did you get it?" Carley asked bluntly not wanting to spend any more time than she needed to with the surly detective.

"Here," Ron said as he handed Carley a wrinkled brown envelope. Carley took it and quickly emptied the contents into her hand. It was a computer security access card.

"What's this?" She enquired as she studied it, "You were supposed to get the file!"

"I had a tough enough time of getting that," Ron protested. "That file is in McNeill's personal drive. That card will get you in."

"How am I supposed to get in there?"

"I'm sure you'll find a way sweetness," Ron sneered.

"Fuck sakes! And the other thing?" A frustrated Carley replied.

Ron stared at her uncooperatively, displeased that he was bowing to Carley's wishes.

"Carmon!" Carley barked.

Reluctantly, Ron dipped his hand into his pocket and removed the Gold Locket Necklace, holding it in front of Carley's face indignantly. She stared at it for a moment, admiring its unusual beauty, then she attempted to pull it away from Ron, but he held on.

"You've got what you wanted, now you keep your mouth shut!" Ron warned. "That goes for that boyfriend of yours too!"

"Whatever," Carley dismissed, but Ron grabbed her arm tightly as she attempted to leave.

Fear filled Carley as she tried to break loose from Ron's steel fisted grip. Ron had had a reputation for being a violent bully and he was feared by the most stalwart of street thugs. She turned back and looked at him, trying to mask her trepidation, as he moved his thick fingers up behind her neck and forcing her closer to him.

"Maybe you do one more thing for me, like the old days," Ron grinned. "You used to love to swallow."

Carley exhaled slowly as she turned and moved in closer to him, staring him in the face with abhorrent disgust.

"Does it make you feel strong to talk to me like that?" Carley questioned, as she removed her phone from her pocket, pressed stop and then playback. Once again Ron's voice played back; *'You used to love to swallow...'*

"Don't you ever talk to me like that again. Or you'll find this on your Facebook page. Cunt," Carley threatened.

Ron retreated sheepishly as Carley exited the car, slamming the door on Ron's flabbergasted reaction. She marched off across the solemn car park, smiling proudly at her newly discovered defiance.

~

Carley could see the staff entrance to the Scotland Yard building, her vision obscured only slightly as she hid behind several large refuse bins. She had spent the best part of two hours cowering behind the metallic behemoths that housed fermenting trash, watching for the right person to leave the building. The cleaning crews had finished their shifts and one by one began to leave the building, and Carley knew she had to spot the one who would fit her height, build, hair colour and facial features. That way she could enter and blend in as one of the non-descript cleaning staff and get up to McNeill's office without being detected. She felt her chances getting slimmer by the minute as she eagerly watched the unassuming aluminium glass door as it slid open producing another person who was either too short, too tall, looked nothing like her or was a man.

The cold night air began to invade her flimsy chiffon dress, sending goose bumps along her already tense spine. Perhaps it was time to abandon her pursuits, return to Nick and tell him that she had failed to help him. She would then have to accept that he might never want to see her again, and the feeling seemed to find an overwhelming sense of woe that pieced her resolve like a bleak spectre. She felt like falling to the floor and crouching in self-degradation, feeling at one amongst the garbage. But then the door slid open once more and she didn't even bother to look intently, apart from a fleeting glance in the direction of the retiring worker. Something about this one registered her attention and Carley stood up gazing intently at her. The woman was slightly taller, but not by much, of similar build, and had slick pulled back blonde hair. She was a perfect match and Carley beheld her inane dress sense. The woman wore figure-hugging black denim, a transparent white blouse that only slightly veiled a red lace bra, wrapped in a brown suede hipster. Carley couldn't help but admire the ensemble and couldn't have done better herself. The woman was a mirror image of her and she watched as the woman returned her security pass into a large leather bag. Carley watched as she passed in front of her and strode down the street. She summoned all her courage and quickly followed after her.

Carley kept a safe distance but did not let the woman out of her sights as she rounded a corner. Carley quickened her pace as she did not want to lose her, and as she came around the corner, she noted that the woman had disappeared. Carley searched about frantically, and then stopped on the sight of the brightly lit staircase descending into the Tube station. She quickly hopped along, then hurried down the stairs hoping that she had not lost the woman to a departing train. Carley reached the metal turnstile and speedily swiped her Oyster travel card and barged through the bar, plodding toward the descending escalator and skipping on the cascading steps. As the escalator began to descend, Carley spotted her. She was near the bottom reaching the end. Carley doubled her efforts and began to race downward, careful not to lose her footing and tumble.

As Carley reached the bottom she looked frantically to each platform – one was going east and the other west. She threw caution to the wind and opted to go left on to the east platform. She scampered through the archway, onto the long winding platform as it gently curled alongside the charcoal coloured track. She swiftly threw her head in each direction trying to spot her target, but she was nowhere on the platform! The wind on the platform picked up as an approaching train produced a vortex. Carley turned as she realised that the train was approaching the neighbouring platform going in the opposite direction. With a determined vigour, she hastily spun around and bolted across the middle concourse between the subterranean platforms. Almost leapfrogging, Carley took the biggest steps that she could, covering as much ground. The train whizzed along the platform and Carley could see the dazzling windows sail past through the small tunnel entrance to the platform. Panting like a sprinter she emerged onto the platform, ruthlessly searching for her prey. The doors of the train opened, and Carley spotted her prey waiting for alighting passengers to disembark, before stepping on to the carriage. Carley wasted no time and scrambled toward the carriage as the shrill bells signalled the closing of the doors. Carley launched herself through the air, almost fly-tackling the boarding passengers, including the blonde woman, causing her to fall to the train floor, with Carley landing on top of her.

"What is wrong with you?" The blonde woman protested at Carley, as she sat up briskly, trying to recompose and gather the elements that had fallen from her bag and strewn across the train floor.

"I'm so sorry," Carley lamented, vigorously trying to help the woman return the contents of her life into her bag. "Let me help you."

But Carley's offer was met with scorn as the woman, tugged her belongings away from Carley and promptly got to her feet.

"Nice jacket," Carley smiled as the woman straightened her attire and moved to the end of the carriage as far away from Carley as possible.

Carley carefully rose to her feet as the other passengers returned to the mundanity of their commute. She turned to face the black tunnel fissures sweeping by on the outside of the train carriage. In her hand, she clasped the staff access card she needed to get into Scotland Yard.

~

Scotland Yard was deserted at 3am apart from the scant service personnel that occupied a few desks. Carley wasted no time in assuming the alter ego that she had worked so hard in acquiring. She donned an unflattering grey polo shirt embroidered with *Clean Angels*, that she had liberated from her victim's locker and wore it over her ripped denim that exposed a portion of her upper thigh below her buttocks, hoping no one would notice. She despised the cleaner's uniform and couldn't wait to disrobe from it, but it was necessary to maintain her charade and accomplish her solitary mission.

Carley wheeled the cumbersome cleaning caddy into the large service lift and took a deep breath as she watched the doors shut behind her. She watched the illuminated panel display the floor numbers as she ascended and eventually it settled on the fourth floor, coming to a juddering halt. The doors shuddered open and before her lay the entire CID floor. Tentatively, she pushed the cart forward. This was her first visit to the fourth floor, although she had been to the second where she met with Miles Munroe, something she now regretted. But deep down, on some level, it was an action that made her see how Nick had truly felt about her. In the diner, the previous day she saw something in him that she had not seen before – and that was hurt. She felt terrible that she had to go to such drastic lengths to see it, but she needed to. She needed to see that he cared and that she wasn't just there when he was alone and needed the warmth of her pungent presence next to him. She wanted to see that he felt something – maybe even love. It wasn't that she needed to hear it, because he would not say it. That much she knew was true, but she could read him pretty well and she read his heartbreak at her going to Munroe. It was a wound that she had to administer, just to see if he would bleed for her. And he did. Now she would have to nurse that wound back to health, she thought to herself, as she walked passed a desk that displayed the nameplate *DC Narendra Shankar*. She smiled proudly as a sense of allegiance produced warm emotions of determination. She was going to do this.

She parked the cart up against a glass partition in front of the office door that displayed the words *Chief Superintendent Rory F. McNeill*. She had never met the man, but something in his name made her feel uneasy. She reached into the storage drawer and produced a set of keys with the worn tag *Fourth Floor* written in barely legible black handwriting, and began trying the different keys, hoping that one would strike true and open the door.

Carley had tried eight different keys until one seemed to turn the lock only halfway, jamming on a formidable sticky turn. Carley placed all of her might trying to turn the lock, but it would not budge.

"Pull on it," A voice echoed from behind a dimly lit desk. "The Superintendent's door gets quite sticky. Pull it then turn the key."

Carley could not make out whom the voice had belonged to, but she welcomed the much-needed advice and followed it. The door popped opened on the action and Carley pushed her way into the office quickly as her heart thumped with excitement. She realised that she was risking so much as she moved quickly to plant herself in front of the PC on McNeill's desk. Security wasn't as strong as she anticipated, but then nobody in their right mind would risk breaking into Scotland Yard anyway.

Carley tapped on the keyboard, and the PC awoke from its slumber as the screen lit up. She then removed the access card, that she obtained from Ron, and inserted into the card reader as the machine prompted. The screen went straight to the desktop with the picture of a French pug. Carley winced at the sight of the smug looking animal. She placed her hand on the mouse and moved the cursor to a file folder and clicked it open. Then she typed the words, Khan into the search bar and clicked enter. A list of files dropped down on screen in front of her. Carley scrolled carefully through them and then paused on one of them titled *A_Khan_468942_4th July 2014*. Carley double-clicked on the file as a dialog box prompted: *Encrypted file – Password required.*

"Fuck sakes," Carley muttered under her breath, searching around the room looking for a clue to the password. Carley then stopped as she realised what it could be and 'minimised' the file window, staring at the desktop picture, squinting at the screen trying to make out the letters on the name tag. She carefully made out the word that the letters formed and then typed the word *Winston* into the password box. The file opened. In front of Carley sat the frozen image of a dispossessed Adilaah Khan. Somehow the grainy image haunted her.

The grey morning light was beginning to

protrude through the closed blinds and Carley realised that time was escaping her. She turned her attention at the clock on the PC. It was almost 5:30am. Quickly she removed a flash drive from her pocket and inserted into the USB drive, and then copied the file. She watched the progress bar, poking her head up from behind the P.C, ensuring that her presence had not been detected.

"Carmon!" Carley exclaimed, frustrated at the slow pace of the computer. Suddenly the outline of a figure appeared outside the door to the office. Hastily she dropped down to the floor and tried to eject the flash drive, but the file copy was incomplete.

"Fuck sakes," Carley cursed.

McNeill stood before his office door in befuddlement, staring at the cleaning cart parked outside it. He approached it cautiously inspecting its curious position. He could hear a commotion originating from within the office. He placed his hand on the door, but it was locked. There was a stirring in his gut and he became suspicious. McNeill inserted his key slowly into the door and pulled then pushed it after unlocking it, and dubiously entered. McNeill surveyed the dark cold office. At the opposite end a window sat ajar and the blinds flapped in the ensuing wind. McNeill moved quickly through the office toward the window. He shut it with vigour and then a brush of movement alerted him from behind. He spun around but the was nobody there. But somebody had been. He could sense it. Someone had disturbed the perfect equilibrium of his office. The intrusion made him feel out of place in his own office. Then he looked at his desk. It was not as he left it.

Carley had barely enough time to remove the flash drive, lock the door and hide under the desk. Her heart pounded in her chest as she heard the door open and somebody enter. It must have been McNeill, but she could not tell. She had managed to open the window as part of a hastily hashed plan that she had concocted as she waited for the drive to conclude. She hoped that the window would distract him long enough so that she could stealthily crawl out from behind the desk and be out the door before it closed, and he turned around. True to form McNeill went for the window, and with all the courage she could muster she stealthily scampered from under the desk and slid out the door just as it shut, and he turned around. But he knew that someone had been in his office. But it did not matter. A few minutes later she was back on the street, and she tossed the unflattering cleaning uniform into the bin.

She had done it. She had got Nick what he needed to restore his faith in her.

And in them.

16

Nick savoured the Jack Daniels as the gentle burn of the bourbon swilled down his parched throat. He had missed the flavour and intensity of the drink that previously, he would consume by the bottle. But tonight, he needed some respite and the sweet fragrant liquor was enough to do just that. Carley had told him to meet her at their usual wobbly table in The Green Man. The night was quiet and there were only a few regulars assuming their usual positions at the bar and at the tables. Nick watched as Stewart seemed more engrossed in two girls seated at the bar sipping sparkling champagne from long stem glasses, interspersed with gleeful giggling. They seemed out of place in a pub like this, and perhaps they had come across town to see how the other half drinks. Nick stared at them, thinking they were probably more suited to a bar in Chelsea, rather than the salt-of-the-earth joint that this was. But still, Stewart seemed to be entranced by them, smiling like a giddy schoolboy, topping up their drinks with persistence, perhaps hoping that he could get in their posh knickers.

Nick wasn't sure why he had even come tonight, but he was curious. She had told him that she could help and set things right. Although he wasn't sure what that would mean exactly. He was still determined to bring Adilaah's real killer to justice, but for that he needed evidence, and even if he had that, he knew he was pitting himself against everything and risking it all. She said that she could help and so he told her that he needed the details of Adilaah's statement when she was questioned after her beating, if it even existed. Nick had to remind himself that he was going on a lead provided by Nadir, a suspect that might have been lying to save his own skin. But his gut told him otherwise. And now Carley was going to do something rash in order to bring him that evidence.

Nick wasn't sure what she even meant when she said she would call on some old favours in to get her hands on what he needed. Her misplaced and skewed loyalty could land her in prison. A sudden feeling of denial shrouded his thoughts and Nick realised he didn't even want to know what she was up to. Judging by her past, that could be anything, often dubious and illegal. Better that he didn't know. Especially in as, this is how this whole Tyson mess got started in the first place. She was trying to earn his favour. And perhaps he was done with her favours.

But then just as he gulped that remaining contents of his drink, a plastic object was slid on the table in front of him. Nick looked up to see Carley, standing proudly before him with a look of grandeur.

"What's this?" Nick enquired with a look of concern.

"It's what you wanted," Carley declared.

Nick picked up the plastic flash drive and examined it. "How did you?" He muttered.

Carley rolled her eyes unwilling to reveal her exploits, and she plonked down into the seat opposite him, taking the weight from her tired loins and exhaling deeply.

"I don't know what to say," Nick said softly, as he fondled the flash drive in his fingers and caught Carley's gaze. She did make this better and he wanted to tell her that she did well, and that he had forgiven her for going to Munroe. But he could not. The words refused to come, and he just stared at her with a vacant smile. Carley sat back quietly. She did not need his words. She knew she had redeemed herself and she knew how he felt despite his lack of words. That was enough for her, and she reached down into her coat pocket and produced the Gold Locket necklace and slid it across the table cupped in her hand.

"Give me your hand," Carley offered.

Nick reluctantly placed his hand on the table and opened his palm. Carley opened her cupped fist and released the necklace into his, caressing it as she removed it. Nick looked at it with remorse. That necklace was the harbinger of doom.

Everyone who touched it seemed to have met their untimely end. Even though he was happy to see it back with him, he could not help but think he wanted to be rid of it too.

"Munroe has nothing on you now," Carley declared. "My confession never mentioned you. Just Ron."

She stared at the necklace longingly. Nick focused on the necklace that sat in the palm of his hands and then he turned his attention toward Carley. He could sense that she saw the necklace as means for redemption, as a chance to be on the same par as Adilaah or even his mother. To her it meant that she could be vindicated and finally feel something that she had never felt before – to belong and be valued.

"Come here," Nick said as he succumbed. "I want you to have this." He leaned forward, undid the clasp and placed the jewel around her firm neck.

Carley could hardly contain her delight and wrapped her arms around his head as he retreated and kissed him on the lips. This time the kiss was different. It wasn't filled with passion or lust, but love, and it lingered as they savoured it, eyes shut and inhaling each other's essence. For the first time Nick didn't want to pull away. It felt special and he did not want to fight it like he had so many times before. His heart was pounding, and he did not want to let her go.

"You know I..." Nick stuttered, but his words could not emulate how he felt.

"Words don't come that easy for either of us, do they?" Carley replied, smiling at him.

"Unspoken words," Nick said as he reflected. He had said the same words to Adilaah once.

"Sometimes they just get in the way," Carley replied.

~

Nick sat in front of his compact dining table in front of his laptop. He was sure that Carley would have wanted to spend the night, but he needed to analyse the contents of the flash drive she had brought him. So, he left her to make her own way home while he returned to his apartment. The taste of Jack Daniels lingered on his palette and he craved another drink, but he resisted. He needed to be completely lucid for this vital information on the drive. Nick inserted the drive into the USB port and the file marked *A_Khan_468942_4th July 2014* appeared on screen, and he clicked open the file as a feeling of foreboding enraptured him.

A series of photographs and scanned documents appeared as mini icons on the screen and Nick slowly opened each one. The first was an image of Adilaah's arm, bruised with red and blue blotches. Nick perused further, revealing a close-up of bruised abdomen, then a cut eye and swollen purple left eye.

Nick clicked open a report and read through. He had read many reports in his short career but none of them made him feel sick as this one did. With each line of the report, the glaring truth tore a strip out of his doubt and tolerance for her unfortunate fate.

It read;

Victim severely beaten with bruising over 70% of body.

Victim has significant abdominal haemorrhaging and vaginal tearing.

Pregnancy test: positive.

Aggravated, Nick closed the file and then opened another. Nick felt his heart sink as he witnessed Adilaah's dour terrified expression, as the video file began to play.

The voice of a female Constable filled the speakers as the camera stayed firmly on Adilaah.

"Miss Khan, I realize that this must be difficult for you, but I must stress the need to complete this report in earnest."

"Yes," Adilaah mumbled barely able to open her mouth to form words from her injuries.

"I understand your inability to speak, so you can just agree or disagree to any of these questions, but if you can provide any details, we would appreciate it," The Constable said objectively.

Nick paid close attention as Adilaah nodded.

"You've indicated to the investigating Officer that you were attacked in your home, but you refuse to name your attacker," The Constable continued.

Adilaah remained still and silent.

"Are you protecting somebody? Is it because you fear a further attack or reprisals?"

Adilaah vehemently shook her head in denial, as tears began to form in her eyes.

"Miss Khan the nature of your injuries suggests an attack of the most violent nature. By protecting the attacker you risk this happening to other individuals, innocent people whose trauma or even death might be prevented by your testimony."

Adilaah began to well up as the tears began to stream from her traumatised face, and Nick could barely contain his own remorse for her predicament.

"You don't have to make this so hard on yourself. Your attacker is known to you?" The Constable probed further.

Adilaah nodded reluctantly.

"Is it a family member?"

Adilaah nodded again, as Nick took a deep breath, his heart breaking for Adilaah's torment.

"Now take your time," The Constable coaxed, "Can you tell me who it is? You are safe here. No one can hurt you."

Adilaah vehemently shook her head in denial unable to let the truth reign free.

"Miss Khan please. You've been raped. You've been beaten and been in coma for three days. Don't let this person get away with this unpunished. Is this really the person you want to be protecting? Find the strength to face this, to face your attacker…" The Constable convinced.

Adilaah sat silently as she looked up to the camera. Her eyes made contact with Nick's as her might rose from within, encouraging her to utter the all-important truth.

This time the words resonated with Adilaah on a primal level and suddenly she found doubtless resolution and boundless strength. She opened her mouth, struggling to pronounce the words, but then uttered them nevertheless.

"My father. My father did this to me!" Adilaah lamented, seething with rage and scorn.

Nick clicked on the mousepad and paused on the image of Adilaah's distraught frozen face. He stared into her anguished hollow eyes as her ghostly image stared back at him reaching out like a spectre from beyond the grave.

17

Sleep evaded Nick as he lay in bed wrestling with the image of Adilaah's forlorn and embattled face. It haunted him to the core, upsetting his conscience and constitution. The rape had clearly happened after they had separated. He had told her to go back to her father and the life that came with it. He told her that she was more in love with that, than him. They were words said in anger. He did not mean them. He knew that she loved him as much as he loved her, but he wanted to have her all to himself. Now he regretted those harsh, selfish words. For she was clearly not in love with the brutality and fear that was her existence. In him she saw an opportunity to have some semblance of a normal life. Most of all, to have love.

Nick closed his eyes as he tried to find solace in that thought. He had been her only love. Her only hope. He turned over to his side and pulled the covers over his head as a means of escape from the precluded reality that was his bedroom and travelled back to another time.

Then there she was, holding a book in her

hands. Her face was plump and healthy, full of youthful exuberance and life, free from the purple swollen bruises that bore the brunt of her father's onslaught. Nick's breathing shallowed and he focused on the memory of her words:

Thou hast said that Thou wilt torment me,
But I shall fear not such a warning.
For where Thou art, there can be no torment,
And where Thou art not, how can such a place exist?
The rotating wheel of heaven within which we wonder,
Is an imaginal lamp of which we have knowledge by similitude.
The sun is the candle and the world the lamp,
We are like forms revolving within it.
A drop of water falls in an ocean wide,
A grain of dust becomes with earth allied.

"Thou wilt torment me. But I shall fear not such a warning. For where thou art, there can be no torment," Nick whispered the words back from memory. He had heard Adilaah recite those words and so did Nadir.

Nick sprung out of bed as though he had become possessed by a demon and raced naked through his hallway and across to a pile of books unceremoniously stacked in the corner of his living room. He waded through each title, tossing the ones that did resound with his search. Then suddenly he stumbled across the book that he was searching for, reading the title as he examined it:

The Rubaiyat of Omar Khayyam. It was still in its original ribbon wrapping, as he gently caressed it stirring up the memory of how he received it from Adilaah.

~

Adilaah stood in a hallowed light almost in the same spot where Nick was kneeling over his pile of books. She placed the white leather-bound book in his hands as if she was handing over something sacred and of value. Then she handed him a card.

"Read the inscription," Adilaah said affectionately. Nick opened the card it read:

Don't remember the last day,
Don't cry for the future,
In the past and in the future don't believe,
Live today and don't lose in the wind your life.

Nick sighed heavily as the words were written for him to read that very moment, in his present state.

Then he remembered asking, "Can I open it?", as he beheld the book, and she replied,

"Open it when I'm gone."

~

But now it was time Nick thought, as he pulled the ribbon off and let it fall casually to the floor. He carefully opened the book as the flood of anticipation overwhelmed him. He studied the first page and he recognised Adilaah's handwriting. Her words came to life as he read them:

My escape is my journal and its words. The poems are my carriages, transporting me away from my father's hand.

Nick turned to another page.

I fear for my life. I think he is going to kill me.

Then he briskly turned to another page and more of her confessions saw light;

He told me he loves me, and I wish I could have said the same. I wish I could love him like a normal girl. I am so trapped.

Nick turned his attention to the facing page,

I wish he would kill me. I can't stand this anymore. I wish I were dead!

Nick slammed the book shut. He could take no more of her torment. The book was full of Adilaah's harrowing experiences, and he hated the fact that he was powerless to do anything about it while she was alive. She had come to him and she needed him to help her escape her situation. But he had done nothing. He just wanted to love her and have her for himself without regard for what she was going through and how impossible it was for her to escape. Instead he turned her away and sent her back to her tormentor. He was just as guilty as the one who had smashed her skull in, for she came to him for protection. She knew that they wouldn't dare harm a policeman, particularly one that had such a history with the family. But for Mahmoud Khan such indiscretions could not go unpunished and as soon as he regained control over her after their affair, he beat her and raped her to remind her that he was the master in her life, one that she could never escape. One that she still could not. For all he knew, she might have tried to contact him, after the abortion, but he was submerged in his work. He used ambition as an antidote to the heartbreak and loss that he felt for her. By that point Carley was firmly in his life.

18

Nick didn't really want to do it but his new partner, DCI Ron Allen had told him that this was an important lead and he needed to follow it up. Nick was nervous. He had never met nor interrogated an informant before, and it's not like they taught this in a class at the academy. This part of the job took instinct, tenacity and maturity. It came with experience, years of dealing with these kinds of people on the street. Many of these people were simply looking to trade useless information for money or protection because that were in a jam and could lose their lives without a new-found allegiance with a police constable. This why Ron sent him on his own, to see if he could succeed. A test to see if he had the right stuff that equated to detective material. And Nick knew that he had to impress his new partner.

Ron had only given him a brief description of the informant. All he said was she was blonde with a 'fuck-off' attitude and that he would know her when he saw her. As he approached the door to the café, Nick paused and took a deep breath.

He was nervous yet, strangely excited. This is what he had always wanted to do since being a little boy and seeing his heroes on so many TV cop shows. He pushed through the weathered wooden door and was greeted by the intoxicating aroma of fried eggs and grilled bacon. The smell filled his nose and travelled straight down to his stomach awakening a fervent hunger pang. It was almost lunchtime and the cafe was almost full, so the place must have been good, and judging by the wonderful aromas, he didn't have to guess why.

Nick carefully surveyed the place, noting any suspicious persons or reactions. His training had started to fuel his natural instinct and strangely the assertion and authority in his presence instantly made the onlookers realise he was a detective, albeit a trainee. He looked around slowly, carefully analysing the appearance and body language of each individual, but none seemed to fit the description of his informant. He made another sweep, but this time he caught sight of someone who had occupied a table by herself. She had her head buried in her arms, lying face down on the table, and did not see Nick walk in, but on his second pass she clocked him and realised he was her contact. Their eyes met and he slowly moved toward her table. She watched him strangely transfixed. She was wearing a scruffy bobble hat, a worn sweat shirt over a tight skirt and fish net stockings, covering a skinny, pouting figure. Nick gazed at her too, as he moved to confront her, catching a portentous stare from the greasy cook who Nick could only guess was the owner. She removed her bobble hat to reveal tightly pulled back platinum blonde hair, and Nick couldn't help but admire her emerald blue eyes set in her white slightly freckled face.

"Ron with you?" She asked, somewhat bluntly.

"No. I'm alone," Nick replied dryly as he sat down.

"But I needed to talk to him," She said impatiently and began to fidget with the overly long sleeves on her grubby sweat shirt, scratchy at her forearms.

Nick could tell that she had been using for a while, and she was on a solid come down. She was edgy and twitchy, and it wouldn't be long before she would need the welcome relief only the cooked contents of a needle would provide.

Just then a middle-aged wrinkled leather-faced waitress appeared before them with a less than courteous manner.

"You gonna eat?" She barked, as she stared at Nick's companion with outright revulsion, making it clear that she was not welcome.

"All day breakfast, please," Nick answered quickly, diffusing the situation.

"What about her?" The waitress replied with indignance, hardly making any eye contact with the girl.

"She'll have the same," Nick replied briskly, his manner dismissing the impertinent woman, "And tea," he shouted as she stormed off. Then he smiled at the girl across from him and she cracked an empty smile in return, an expression she had clearly not used in a while.

Nick watched her manner and under the objectionable junkie exterior there was something else, an enduring palpable sense of herself that had fallen prey to something which she had no choice over. But she would never let it overtake her. In her eyes she bore the last vestige of her unwavering strength. And Nick could see that. Perhaps he was the only one who could see it. The waitress didn't and judged her otherwise, seeing only a street skank that was unwelcome in the cafe. Though, Nick had made a strange connection with her, and maybe it was because he felt sorry for this creature who was clearly a survivor that now seemed like a damsel in need of rescuing. In any event, this personal connection would help him pry the information from her. But something told Nick that she would be more than just an important informant that could provide the valuable inroads into a notorious gang leader and criminal. She would be something more than that.

"Nick," he announced gallantly to her, as she relaxed and composed herself.

"Carley," She said blissfully.

~

Carley couldn't stop thinking about the events of the night as she sat at the deserted bus stop patiently awaiting the number one-two-one bus. But the wait did not bother her as her thoughts were filled by Nick and the necklace around her neck. Uncharacteristically she felt like a schoolgirl besotted by a boy and revelling in an adolescent daze. It had been a long twenty-four hours, and even though she ached from fatigue, it was worth it.

Carley stretched out her tired arms and rolled her stiff neck, massaging some relief into them. A figure appeared from the mild night air and sat slowly and calmly on the red moulded plastic seat. Carley immediately retracted her arms, permitting the stranger enough space to sit comfortably next to her in the compact space. He wore a large black hooded sweatshirt over baggy denim and white trainers. They looked expensive, Carley thought, but paid no attention to it. The route she lived on was full of unsavoury and weird characters, and by all accounts she used to be one. She reached in between her bosom and removed the necklace, admiring its alluring beauty and the significance it held for her. The hooded figure caught glimpse of the necklace, but as Carley turned to face him he turned away, returning to his frozen stature, with head drooped forward and hands buried deeply in his pocket.

Carley looked around and the streets were deserted, as a strange sense of apprehension seemed to descend upon her. She could not understand why, but she suddenly felt the figure next to her meant her harm and that she was in mortal danger. She looked at her watch, and then slowly turned her attention to the hooded figure, but she could not see his face. Her unease became more prevalent as she began to rock back and forth, not knowing whether to run or wait for the bus.

Suddenly in the distance the headlights of the red double-decker illuminated the dark lifeless street and Carley breathed a sigh of relief. She sprung to her feet and moved closer to the edge of the pavement, signalling its stop. The bus came to a serene halt in front of the stop and Carley could barely wait for the doors to slide open before she flung herself inside and tapped her Oyster travel card on the reader. Hastily, she headed up the winding stairs to the second deck and plonked down into a seat, watching the stairwell, to see if her hooded companion would follow. There was no sign of him and Carley breathed a sigh of relief as the bus groaned off.

Carley watched as the bus made its way along its usual route, resting her head on the window. The vibration on her temple helped relax her and her eyelids began to become heavy and droop slowly. An array of street lights and illuminated shop facades paraded by as Carley fell into a trance-like half sleep. But she awoke with a start as the familiar surrounding became unfamiliar and she realised she had gone passed her stop.

Quickly she pressed the button to get the bus to stop.

The bus began to slow down, and Carley rose from her seat, bobbing around as the top deck swayed and she plodded down the stairs in an exhausted amble, finally reaching the double doors in the middle of the coach, ready to disembark.

Then there he was! She spotted him sitting in the rear of the lower deck, his head lowered, and face unrecognizable. Carley panicked as the middle doors slid open, and the hooded figure rose to his feet too. She froze in front of the open doors and the chilly wind filled the bus. She tentatively looked back at the hooded figure as he had stopped by his seat too, his face still obscured.

"Are you getting off love?" The bus driver bellowed.

Carley sprung from the bus hurriedly and the doors closed behind her. She galloped away in the direction of her shared house. It wasn't far, but it was at least ten to twelve minutes walking, and in this neighbourhood, nobody would open the door if she suddenly screamed out in peril. She ran as fast as she could as the bus sailed past her. In her panic she couldn't tell if the hooded figure had alighted or remained on board. He was probably still on board and she was just being paranoid. He was just some innocent man who was too shy and that had made him seem sinister.

Her tired mind was just playing tricks on her she thought. How foolish.

But then the bus slowed and stopped ahead, and Carley froze. How could this be? It never stopped unless it was at a designated stop. Unless the bus driver had come face-to-face with the same man that gave an otherwise streetwise Carley the chills, and he stopped to let him off, not wanting to risk his own skin.

Carley watched as the doors opened and almost as if it was in slow motion, the hooded figure alighted, one foot at a time and then stood shrouded in shadow a few metres before her. The bus sped off and Carley gulped as she looked around anxiously. The figure just stood and watched her.

Then she hurriedly darted left into one of the small alleyways between the large foreboding houses of the street. Carley ran as fast as she could, using the shadows for cover and searching for a place to hide from her pursuer. Before her stood a sealed archway on the side of a house and she planted herself in it, holding her breath and trying to silence her panting. As she quietened, the eerie silence of the street pervaded, and she popped her head out slowly trying to see if the hooded figure was still on her tail. Carley reached into her pocket and removed her phone, dialling Nick's number and holding the phone to her ear but got the voice of his answerphone.

"Fuck sakes!" Carley muttered under her breath and hung up.

She took a deep breath, shutting her eyes and summoning enough courage to endure the rest of her journey home.

But then just as she stepped out from under the cover of darkness, he appeared like a hooded gory spectre, and grabbed her.

Carley struggled and tried to find the force of her voice, but his bony fingers formed a guard over her mouth, obstructing any sound and stifling her breathing. Then she saw it, glistening in the moonlight, a bright long sabre that thrust downward. She used her hands to block it, but nothing could yield its velocity. She felt it conquer her soul like a foreign invader, interrupting the flow of her life force. It wasn't even the wound that mattered, it was more the realisation of the end of mortality – the end of her life.

Her attacker removed the blade and then reinserted with more vigour and it plunged higher up closer to her heart.

Carley felt warm fluid travel up the back of her throat and spurt out of her mouth. She struggled, clasping the hood with her hand to reveal his face. Another hand launched up for his throat, but he fought her off and she could only grip on a wrist chain as she fell backward. But she held on and locked the chain in her fist as she fell to the floor.

For a moment she lay on the floor and stared up

at her attacker, and he stared back at her. Her eyes became blurry and uncontrollable fatigue began to close in, but the image of his face was imprinted on her mind. He tried to pry her fist open, but she would not let him. Something must have disturbed him. A passerby or an onlooker. Whatever it was, he quickly fled.

So many thoughts passed through her mind, as she lay there. Her mum and dad. Her school. Her first time with Peerless. Tyson. And of course, Nick. He was her final thought. She felt loved. She would miss him and all the little things. But she could leave this life behind because she knew love and she had given it selflessly.

Her eyes became heavy. Then they closed.

19

Nick stood under the hot spot lamps over the gurney that held Carley's body. The light blue cloth that covered her was wet with blood, fresh from her inflicted wounds. Nick was transfixed by it feeling like an embalmed corpse himself. He looked her up and down, full of disbelief that Carley lay under it. His mind was blank. He didn't know what to think or what to feel. Only, a few hours earlier he had been with her and she had sat right before him. She was as happy as he had ever seen her. He felt like they had truly turned a corner and he could tell her how he felt. The conflict had subsided, but how ironic that just as they found the truth and solace in each other, she was dead. He had lost her forever, never able to sound the words of pent up emotion that finally liberated itself. But still, even the thought of that made him feel nothing. The truth was that he was empty – devoid of any emotion. He had nothing left to give after the tumultuous set of emotions and experiences that had occurred. Maybe he was now a true detective, the man that everybody expected him to be, as his father had said to him.

This emptiness was what he needed to finish this thing. To do what it took without the complications of obligation, anger and grief. He knew what he needed to do, to bring it all down. For Adilaah. For Carley.

Aisha appeared before Nick with her usual casual indignance at the corpse that lay in the lab. But somehow, she stemmed most of her blatancy and displayed an air of compassion and emotion as she took hold of the cover sheet, ready to unveil the body. She looked at Nick woefully as he gave her the nod to proceed, and Aisha slowly pulled the cover over, revealing Carley's face.

Nick stared at Carley's face blankly. "How did she die?" He said quietly.

"Knife wounds. Double entry to the abdomen. Cardiac arrest on the street…" Aisha said as she looked at Nick, realising her blunt prognosis was about someone Nick cared about.

"Sorry. I forgot you were close," She apologised. "She tried fighting back. Found this tightly wrapped in her hands."

Aisha showed Nick an evidence bag containing the Moon and Star Emblem wrist chain, as she removed it and displayed it to Nick. Nick took it in his hands and studied it.

"D-N-A has a match, but the file seems to be sealed. Doesn't make sense," Aisha pondered.

"Yes, it does. Perfect sense," Nick announced furtively as he clasped the blood stained Moon and Star Emblem chain tightly in his fist, almost cutting through his skin, and placing it in his pocket. He looked back at Carley, gazing at the Gold Locket necklace still around her neck.

"I was going to process that," Aisha blurted.

"Leave it," Nick interrupted. "She deserves to take to with her."

~

"Let her go!" Nick shouted with the full volume of his voice so that Ashraf wouldn't mistake his tone. By now Ashraf had pinned her to the floor beside the bed and in her drunken catatonic state, she was putting up little resistance.

Ashraf had asked his best friend to head across the street for another bottle of cider, and even though he had had enough, Nick never knew when to stop his drinking. Ashraf knew this well and had often plied his friend with alcohol so that he could get him drunk and help him in his sordid exploits.

Today was just like all those other times. They would drive up to the council estates, and Ashraf knew all the right ones, and offer the girls that hung around, bored and with no money, the time of their lives. Vodka, cider, beer, all that they wanted, but not before making a trip through the 'Maccidees' drive-thru. They loved it and it wasn't long before Ashraf and Nick had a reputation. Sometimes there were too many to fit into Ashraf's pimped-up silver Golf GTI, and they had to turn them away. They would sit in the car park of the local park, blasting out R & B and

Rap music, drinking and smoking, making them believe that for today they were living the high life. They knew that they had to play their parts too, for all that excess came with a price, in the form of fondling, groping or a bit of flashing.

But eventually this all became all too tame for Ashraf and he wanted more. Much more. Nick could see it happening. What had started as a bit of adolescent fun, turned into a predatory sport for Ashraf, almost as if the luring of these teenage skanks was the dress rehearsal for something far more malicious and macabre.

Ashraf knew just who to pick. He could seek out and lure the girl who was wayward, had already had a promiscuous reputation, and was estranged from her parents – a bit of an outcast and loner. At the time, Nick dismissed it as his friend wanting to have fun, and that he knew the boundaries. But deep down he knew that Ashraf was capable of so much more. He had seen that dark side on many an occasion and he had tried to stay clear of it.

On that particular day, they had bunked college. They were in their final year so to them it didn't matter much. Ashraf had his sights on one girl in particular – Megan. On the face value, Megan looked like she did not belong on a council estate. She looked prim and proper, conservatively dressed, sweet, kind and pretty. She had auburn red hair with a fresh excitable face and ecstatic laugh that was infectious. But she too had a dark side and that was blatantly apparent when she had a few drinks. The fiery redhead came out of her and she lost all self-control, gaining a reputation for being outright crazy. However, the one thing that Megan never did was let anybody touch her, despite her raucous and raunchy reputation. In fact, she was probably a virgin. Something that Ashraf saw as a challenge. The other thing that sat in contrast to Megan's diametric personality was that she was quite shy and sensitive when she was sober and could hold an intelligent conversation once she came out of her shell. But for some reason she chose to hide that part and let the outlandish aspect dominate. Nick had spent some time talking to her about the loveless environment she grew up in, especially as the alcohol wore off. He felt that perhaps that she masked her true feelings because she was terrified of love and did not know how to give or receive it. Hence the wild party animal triumphed. But Nick wished he could see more of that side of her. He liked it, and he knew she liked him. But there was only one problem. Ashraf liked her too. But not in the same way. He saw her as prey that he could hunt and consume.

Nick knew that Ashraf had sent him out of the room for a reason. Ashraf had often brought girls to these rooms. They had sat above his family's curry restaurant where he took most of his meals.

As he entered the room, he heard Megan's

muffled cries, something that he had heard many times before. Ashraf often got them drunk and forced himself on them. They were always White, and he took a certain pleasure from hearing them whimper and plead. Often, they had passed out and he would have rough intercourse with them, gleefully laughing and then occasionally slapping them in the face. Nick tried to stop his friend but somehow felt powerless to do so. If he intervened, that would place him on the opposite side to Ashraf, and it would jeopardise their friendship and arouse his anger. Deep down Nick despised himself, for he felt he was party to it, an accomplice who could just as easily, be on top of that girl himself.

But this time it was all too much. He knew that Ashraf had purposefully left the door unlocked, and as he entered he saw that Ashraf was between her legs ready to enter her. That was when he shouted, and the grin that Ashraf had on his face turned furtive.

"What?" Ashraf barked as he faced Nick's challenge.

"I said get off her," Nick commanded as he launched forward, lifting Ashraf off Megan and throwing him across the room.

The shock and vigour of his friend's actions took Ashraf by surprise as he tried to compose himself.

"What are you doing? Ashraf questioned his friend's rebuke.

"I'm done with this!" Nick announced loudly.

"Done?" Ashraf sniggered. "But we're best friends."

Nick moved over to Megan and helped her to her feet. He hoped that Ashraf wouldn't try to stop him, as he was much stronger.

"No. We're not," Nick answered bluntly. "This is not what friends do."

Ashraf stared at Nick somewhat bewildered as he led Megan out the door. He couldn't understand why Nick had reacted in that way. He knew his friend was soft-hearted, but he had always counted on his loyalty.

~

Ashraf sat hunched over a table in the empty restaurant, swilling down spoonsful of rich butter chicken and naan bread as Nick pushed the door open and entered. It was no different from when they would spend their days discussing football, wrestling or their favourite TV shows. But now things were different, very different. Ashraf was no longer his friend, but a killer he had come to arrest.

Ashraf did not even lift his head up from his meal, as Nick coolly walked up to him. The restaurant was half baked by the setting sun and Ashraf sat in the dimly lit back end.

Nick ardently placed the Moon and Star Emblem chain on the clothed table in full view of Ashraf as he ominously sat directly before him.

"You lost it the other night," Nick said biliously.

"Good of you," Ashraf taunted, as he gazed at the chain with a wry smile. "A gift from my father. Not as nice as the one you gave Adilaah."

"Why'd you do it? She meant nothing to you," Nick questioned.

"But she did to you," Ashraf retorted. "Besides she meddled in affairs that she shouldn't have. If you left things the way they were meant to be, she'd still be alive."

"And Adilaah? Did she meddle too?" Nick persisted.

"Adilaah betrayed us and everything we stood for," Ashraf lamented.

"Do you stand for murder?" Nick quizzed.

"Do you? You apply your principles when they suit you. Everything I've done was out of honour," Ashraf continued.

"Is that you, or your father speaking?" Nick probed.

"I have my father's respect. I've earned it," Ashraf confirmed.

"If that's how he wants you to earn it, then it's not respect!" Nick declared.

"My father loves me…" Ashraf stuttered.

"Yet he came to me to find Adilaah's killer?" Nick said as he watched his old best friend overcome by his argument.

"My father is a man of god – doing god's work," Ashraf muttered, as his resolve weakened.

"Look what he's done to you. Turned you into a killer. In the end Adilaah wished for death, but at least she tried to live, to love, to be free," Nick said calmly.

Nick paused as he watched Ashraf stare into the warm sunlight flooding into the restaurant.

"He killed you a long time ago," Nick slowly exclaimed. "By turning the boy, I knew, into the man you think he wants you to be. You smashed her skull in, but your father is the real murderer. That's why you wrapped her up…" He continued as he watched tears form in Ashraf's eyes.

"You turned her around because you couldn't face her," Nick said.

"She had so much love to give. I watched him take that all away," Ashraf confessed as he wiped his tears away and recomposed himself.

The two men stood silent for a moment and looked at each other with an unspoken resolve. Despite being on opposite sides, something had been settled between them.

"Ashraf don't make this any harder on yourself," Nick pleaded.

"Nick, I wish things could be different, like when we were boys – simple. I wish the world was simple. But this is all that it is. All it's ever going to be for me," Ashraf spoke as he slowly got to his feet, looking toward the front windows of the restaurant.

"Rabbi-ghfirlee, Rabbi-ghfirlee [O my lord, forgive me! O my lord, forgive me!]," Ashraf repeated as he noted the lines of armed Met

Tactical Officers ready and in position outside, with high powered rifles posed to fire.

"They have shoot to kill orders," Nick advised. "From me."

Ashraf slowly retreated from the table as he realized the gravity of his situation. This was not going to end well for him. Overwhelmed, he turned and bolted toward the rear of the restaurant.

"Be advised, suspect is fleeing on foot to the rear of the building. D-C Shankar in pursuit," Nick blurted into his radio as he raced after Ashraf.

Nick burst through the doors of the kitchen struggling to keep a firm foot on the slippery floor, confronted by befuddled staff. By now Ashraf had scampered passed them and pushed his way through the rear door out into the courtyard.

As Nick caught up to the rear service yard, he watched as Ashraf bolted across the street dodging screeching cars. Nick raced in Ashraf's direction, hopping over the first few cars but then he trapped his foot and fell flat into the roadway, just as a car screeched to a halt. He curled his body protectively, shutting his eyes, just as the car stopped just in front of him.

Ashraf had cleared the curb and made a beeline for the vast green common that straddled the road, racing furiously across the grass. Nick sprung to his feet and pursued, determined not to let him get away.

Nick made out a Met squad car, as it screeched to a halt in the adjacent street. The officer alighted and placed a telescopic rifle on the roof of the car, taking aim at the fleeing suspect. Ashraf was running directly towards him and was firmly in his gun sights. He slowed his pace down as he spotted the officer with the rifle pointed at him.

Ashraf stopped dead and turned to face Nick as he caught up.

Ashraf looked Nick in the eye with an expression of dejection.

"Don't do it," Nick barked, as Ashraf reached into his trouser removing a knife and giving Nick a nod of acceptance. Nick could see that he was not going to come quietly and had accepted his fate.

The officer squeezed the trigger of his rifle and the expelled bullet exploded in Ashraf's chest, launching him to the ground with his knife in hand. Nick caught up to Ashraf's lifeless body, as blood poured from the large cauterized wound.

"Bag the knife. It's wanted in a homicide," Nick announced bluntly to the officers arriving on the scene. He walked off trying to catch his breath.

20

It was hard to tell whether Mahmoud was in prayer or simply waiting for him, Nick thought as he walked into his office. The gates and doors had all been open and the Madrassa was deserted at this time of night. Every sound echoed like a choir of tolling bells, loud and obnoxious. His approach was far from stealth and he could tell Mahmoud was expecting him, however he was unsure what kind of welcome he would receive. But Nick was prepared for anything, even his own demise. A determined and resolute peace had settled over him and now nothing was going to stand in the way of its conclusion, not even his own sense of self-preservation or fear. He felt a strange calm and enlightenment, driven by a higher power. The power of righteousness and love. Perhaps that was the reason that Adilaah appeared in his life, at that wedding on that hotel rooftop to help him fulfil his moral conclusion by serving hers. She was a holy light of sanctity that had appeared to purge all the corrupt and wicked ways that had become so rooted in their constitutions, and by the purity of her love, she sacrificed her life to save their souls.

"You've come for me now have you?" Mahmoud announced loudly from behind his desk, as he watched Nick enter his grand marbled office that resembled a great hall rather than an office. "Like a knight on a holy crusade! Charging your officers to me."

He still had a way with words, Nick thought.

"I've come alone," Nick replied bluntly, in no mood for Mahmoud's theatrics.

"Is he dead?" Mahmoud asked incongruously.

"Shot while fleeing," Nick answered without emotion.

"He was weak. Not like you. You found your conviction," Mahmoud waxed. "You always had respect for me. You should have been the son I deserved. If only you were Muslim."

"You already had the son you deserved," Nick lamented. "But he wanted so desperately to earn your respect that he tried to live like you and be you. And for what? An ideal such as honour," Nick lectured.

"How can you stand there and lecture me about ideals, when it is the very thing that made you who you are. You are part of a generation who have the luxury of preaching about ideals and never having worked for them. You can say these things, but you never have to know the pain of sacrifice in order to protect the very ideals you take for granted. Your father made sacrifices. His entire life just so that you could be standing here."

"Was Adilaah part of that sacrifice?" Nick retorted.

Mahmoud immediately fell silent as Nick finished speaking. He reflected on his actions trying to find the words to qualify his actions.

"Adilaah," Mahmoud spoke calmer and softer, "Was too much like her mother."

Mahmoud leaned forward in his chair and placed his head in his hands, rubbing his face.

"She brought joy to everyone and everything. But naïve to the world and its poison."

"No…" Nick declared diligently. "She was the antidote to it."

Nick stepped up to Mahmoud's desk and delicately placed Adilaah's white leather journal in front of him. Then he turned and walked off.

~

The morning rain had become a light mist that had settled serenely over the gravestones. Nick stood with his hands cupped in reverence in front of him. He had only been here a few days earlier, but now he felt different. A sense of calm had descended over him and his mind was quiet. No barrage of thoughts and neverending questions. Today he was at peace and the events of the last week had found their order. No longer did he feel the churn that made him feel like he was on the wrong side of his own fragmented conscience and morality. He had found a resolve and it was a new feeling. He surveyed the grounds and the tranquillity of the cemetery gardens had a parity to his constitution.

"Adilaah loved you Nick," Fatima announced as she penetrated the silence with her declaration. "In that life of despair, you gave her a few moments of hope and freedom."

Fatima came up and stood beside Nick, as she closed up a large umbrella and looked at the gravestone before him.

"She called out to me. It was a cry for help," Nick spoke softly.

"And in a way you answered that cry," Fatima reassured.

"Unspoken words," Nick muttered.

"Maybe it's time you speak them," Fatima urged as she placed her hand on Nick's shoulder and opened her umbrella as she walked off.

Nick then reached inside his coat pocket and removed a bright white rose and placed it gently on the ground in front of the grave stone.

"I love you," Nick whispered softly as he caressed the inscription: *Here lies Carley Anne Banks.*

~

Miles sat slouched in his usual sloppy manner behind his desk. He sat up as Nick entered and flung an envelope onto his untidy desk.

Adilaah's sweet voice gently echoed enigmatic poetic words like a ghostly narration…

It's early dawn, my love, open your eyes and arise…

"The Tyson case. My full testimony. Adilaah Khan's rape interview. Ashraf Khan's DNA from her murder and his knife in the Carley Banks Murder. It's all in there," Nick declared bluntly and turned, walking out of Miles' office. Miles immediately sat up with surprise and examined the envelope he had been waiting so long for.

~

Gently imbibing and playing the lyre...
In the cold death shrouded mortuary, Nadir's lifeless corpse lay in a body bag.

~

For those who are here will not tarry long...
Ron sat on a bench in the gloomy locker room, flanked by two walls of Lockers, dressed in full Police dress uniform. He polished a nickel-plated handgun to a high finish, then stared at it, absorbing it with foreboding repentance. He grinned at it then without remorse placed it firmly in his mouth and pulled the trigger.

~

McNeil sat down at his desk to begin his day with his usual fervour. Placed squarely in the middle of the desk was a plain brown envelope. He carefully lifted the envelope and emptied the contents out.

A Detective badge slid out. It belonged to DC Narendra Shankar.

McNeil examined the badge. Contempt filled his face.

~

Mahmoud sat in his princely upholstered chair at his desk. His arms lay motionless at his side. Across his wrists, his veins lay exposed; sliced open and pouring ruby red blood.

On the desk, sat Adilaah's Journal and alongside lay an elaborately decorated, Islamic inscribed gold dagger with the blade covered in blood.

And those who are gone will not return.

THE END

SAMESH RAMJATTAN
BE YOUR
HIGHER
SELF
EVERYTHING YOU NEED
TO SIMPLY FIX YOURSELF
IN ONE PLACE

Also by Samesh Ramjattan